THE LAST CHAPLAIN

A NOVEL

By Carl M. White

AUSTIN
BROTHERS PUBLISHING

*Dedicated to
Frances,
my best friend and companion,
always and forever!*

PART ONE

A New Day Sitter

1

THE REFRIGERATOR

Like an inchworm, John worked his way across the floor toward the kitchen. Push the walker ahead, take a step with the good leg, drag and half slide the bad leg. Then push the walker ahead again, on and on, inch by inch.

How simple it used to be—get out of bed, put on slippers and a housecoat, and walk to the kitchen to get a glass of cranberry juice from the refrigerator.

He tried to start every day with a fresh glass of cranberry juice. His wife frequently said that if all she brought home from the store was cranberry juice, John would be happy. She could buy the whole store and forget the cranberry juice, and he would complain.

That was pretty much true. He loved his cranberry juice first thing in the morning, and he wasn't waiting around for Josie to get there to get it for him. He could get it himself— one inch at a time.

John pushed his walker across the grey, limestone floor toward a built-in Sub-Zero refrigerator/freezer unit with red oak doors that matched the cabinets. It was a u-shaped, gourmet quality kitchen with black granite countertops and high-end appliances and finishes. As John approached the refrigerator, he spoke, "Cranberry juice."

The screen on the front of the appliance lit up, and a soft feminine voice responded. "There is one 64-ounce bottle of Ocean Spray Cranberry juice. It is approximately half full. Would you like to know the expiration date?"

It wasn't the fridge talking; it was the house computer system, of which the fridge, the washer and dryer, the dishwasher, the freezer, the heating and air, the TV and the internet and the phone systems, the indoor and outdoor lighting systems, and the window shades and blinds—among other things—were all controlled. John could call up a bath at a precise temperature from his recliner. The grandchildren were really impressed.

Frankie was not. They had come to live in this high-tech wonder of a house nearly six years ago. Frankie died three years later. She never did like the house. She felt like it was watching, listening, like they were never really alone.

"Don't talk to that refrigerator," she would tell John in an exasperated voice.

John figured, why not? For some reason when John talked to the refrigerator, he liked to call it Freda.

"It's not a person," his wife would say. "It's just a computer. Don't treat it like it's real."

John never saw the harm. Now, all these years later, he would rather talk to the refrigerator than just about any of his regular visitors. With Freda, he knew where he stood. There was no ambiguity, no duplicity, no reason to suspect a hidden agenda. He asked for information; Freda gave it.

"Yes, Freda, what is the expiration date of the cranberry juice?" he asked.

Freda answered. "February 3, 2026. John, would you like an inventory of the refrigerator's contents and the expiration dates of items soon to expire?"

"No thank you," John answered.

It would probably be the most delightful conversation he would have all day.

The kitchen door chime sounded. Josie entered in a rush like she did every morning. Josie was a 42-year-old African-American private home healthcare nurse who carried around a few extra pounds on a short, 5 foot 4-inch frame. Because John was between daily caretakers, Josie had to come by every morning to see that he was up, fix breakfast, and tend to his meds.

"Pastor John, now you know the rules. You're not to get out of the bed until someone arrives. You're a fall risk!" she said firmly.

John ignored her. He reached out to open the refrigerator door, and the small juice glass he was also trying to hold fell from his grasp, shattering as it hit the floor.

"You see, Pastor John, that could have been you falling to that floor, and that could have been your hip, or your head, shattering. That's why you're not supposed to get out of the bed without someone here to help you," Josie rattled as she retrieved a broom from the pantry.

John was irritated. He was irritated by the sound of her bossy voice, that he was dependent on help, and that he still couldn't hold on to a small glass, months after his stroke. The truth was the Reverend Doctor John A. Grant was irritated with life.

He was alone. His best friend and wife, Frankie, didn't survive a two-year ordeal with cancer. His four children and five grandchildren were scattered to kingdom come, and he hardly saw them. Thirty-seven years of pastoral ministry had ended in disaster. A stroke had nearly left him an invalid, and he was dependent on the charity of others. To put it in words he would not say aloud—life sucked!

John slowly turned and started moving his six-foot-one frame toward the breakfast table. John didn't carry any additional weight, consistently weighing in at about 150 pounds. He had always taken pride in his physical fitness, though he was never athletic. Today he carried even less weight, down to about 120.

"You not talking today?" Josie asked.

John inched along, silently. "Not to you," he thought to himself.

"Okay, okay, you can keep as silent as you wish. I guess after all those years of preaching you used up all your words and you just don't have any left to say." She was trying to goad him.

John wasn't biting. He just continued along like an inchworm all the way to the table.

Josie was not letting up. "Okay, have it your way. You can be as quiet as a church mouse for all I care, but you are going to listen to me."

She retrieved another glass and reached into the refrigerator to get the cranberry juice. The refrigerator said, "The expiration date on that Ocean Spray Cranberry juice ...

"Hush up! If I want to know the expiration date, I'll look on the label," John spoke up.

"There is no need to be snippy with Freda. She didn't do anything," he thought to himself.

"Oh, oh, I see how it is. You care about the refrigerator, but you won't talk to me!"

John said nothing. Now he was goading her.

Josie put the glass of juice in front of him. "Here's your juice. Now, Pastor, you've got a new day sitter coming this morning. She'll be here in a few minutes. You've got to promise me you'll treat this one nicely. The last three all quit, the third one after two days. Two days! That's a record, even for you."

As Josie talked, she opened her bag to take his vital signs.

"That last girl left here saying that this was a godless house and that you were a crazy man. Now Pastor, we just can't have that." She wrapped a blood pressure cuff around his arm as she spoke.

John thought to himself, "Get me a person with some faith—real faith—not just superstition disguised as faith, and it will all work out."

Josie put down her stethoscope, wrote down his numbers, and took his now empty juice glass and poured more cranberry juice. "Use this to take your meds," as she put down a small paper cup with six pills in it.

There would be more pills at noon, even more at dinner, and yet more at bedtime. This was his life now. Pills in the morning, pills in the evening, pills at suppertime, he thought to himself along with the tune of "Ragtime Dolls."

The back doorbell rang.

"That's her now. I mean it Pastor John; you treat this one right. I'm a healthcare professional, not a caretaker. You've got to make this work." Josie scurried to the back door.

Lisa came in.

She was 31 but looked a little older. She had lived life hard in her younger years, but now, she was settled. She was about five foot seven and could stand to lose a little weight. She had shoulder-length auburn hair that she liked to wear pulled back in a ponytail. She was pretty in a cute sort of way, with a warm, fun-loving kind of smile.

This was a good paying job, though the hours were long. That was fine with her. She did not need idle time.

Plan and fix meals, administer meds, wash clothes, do light housekeeping (there was a regular housekeeper), do the grocery shopping and provide transportation when needed. And all of this was for a retired pastor. She hoped that this old man wouldn't hit on her like her last client, an 80-year-old with octopus arms and hands.

Josie said, "Dr. Grant, this is Lisa Smithy. She is your new day sitter."

Lisa smiled and extended her hand.

John looked up at her, and looked down, not saying anything while reaching out a limp right hand.

Josie, always in a hurry, said, "Come on girl, I'll show you around."

John started eating the cereal and fruit Josie had placed before him while the two women disappeared down the hall to the west side of the house. He reached out and touched his iPad 7 on the table. With a few touches, he had the morning paper before him. For the next 15 minutes, he slowly chewed and read while Josie's irritating voice introduced Lisa to the various features of this high-tech home.

"Smithy," John thought. His mind reached back into his memory of over 25 years as pastor of the large, downtown church. "Smithy. I wonder?" he thought. He knew time was running out and he needed to find someone he could trust.

A few minutes later Josie and Lisa came back into the kitchen.

"You'll find the pantry behind that door, and all you have to do is tell the house system you're out of this item or that, and it will be added to your shopping list. Sync your phone to the system, and the list will be sent to your phone."

"Like Alexa?" Lisa asked.

"Like Alexa on steroids. That computer on the desk is linked to the main house computer. On the pin board behind it is a menu for the next few days and a list of the vendors who service the house. You'll get to make out the next menu. This one you're stuck with."

Josie sighed, "I shouldn't have to tell you all of this. I'm a healthcare professional. Bob Burns will give you more details and take you through the steps of voice recognition so the computer will respond to your commands. In the meantime, you'll just have to ask Pastor John to talk to this blasted machine for you."

Lisa looked at Pastor John, quietly peeling a banana on the other side of the room. She whispered, "Does he talk?"

Josie looked over at him and back at Lisa, whispering back, "Oh yeah, he talks, but you don't listen to everything he says, okay? And you don't have to answer all his crazy questions. You're not being interviewed for this job. It is yours already."

John smiled slightly. His hearing was just fine. And he was going to interview her.

Pastor John and Josie had what appeared to be an adversarial relationship, but down deep he appreciated all she had done for Frankie and for him. On her part, Josie had great admira- tion for Dr. Grant. He was a compassionate man with a great mind. Life had just been hard on him these past few years. Josie had been helping the Grants since Frankie had first gotten ill. She really loved that woman, and she loved the pastor.

But she was a healthcare professional, not a caretaker, and she had other clients to see today. She did not have time to be a tour guide.

"Look," Josie said, "Mr. Burns will be here sometime this morning. He will show you the rest of the house and explain everything else to you. In the meantime," she pointed toward John, "he's all yours. He has had his meds and is Binishing his breakfast. He will want to take a shower. All you'll have to do is lay out some clothes for him and help him with his socks and shoes. By the time he finishes, he'll be worn out and ready to get in his recliner and take a nap.

"Are you good?" Josie asked her.

"I'm good," Lisa said, standing up tall with a confident smile.

"Okay, then. I'm out of here." Josie scurried over to the breakfast table to get her things. "John darling, I'm leaving."

Then she leaned over to John's ear and spoke softly but firmly. "You treat this girl right. We can't do this again."

Josie straightened up, smiled a half sincere smile at John, with a twinkle in her eye. John looked up at her and returned a half sincere smile and the twinkle, and Josie was gone.

The kitchen door chimed as she bolted out. Lisa turned and looked at John. He was back to his banana and reading his iPad as if she wasn't even there. Lisa thought to herself, "I can do this."

2

THE HOUSE

The morning went without a hitch. John said nothing. Lisa said very little. He pointed to the clothes he wanted to wear. John went to the shower.

Lisa went to the kitchen to straighten up and to look at what the menu said lunch was to be. A tomato sandwich, carrot sticks, fruit, low-fat chips. She checked the pantry and the refrigerator, which spoke to her when she opened it.

"John, may I help you locate something?

Lisa said, "Uh, I'm not John, I'm Lisa."

Freda answered, "I'm sorry, I do not recognize this voice."

Lisa took a step back. She wondered if something was going to happen.

Nothing did.

She checked to see that there were tomatoes, mayonnaise, lettuce, carrot sticks and fruit. Satisfied, she shut the door.

Again Freda spoke. "Would you like an inventory of the refrigerator's contents and the expiration dates of items soon to expire?"

From behind her, a man's voice said, "No thank you."

Lisa jumped. Standing behind her at the entrance to the kitchen from the den was Bob Burns. He was short, about five feet six inches tall with a small frame, a nearly bald head with short dark hair on the sides, and intense eyes. At 58, he had learned to always be polite, precise and very business-like.

She had not heard him come in. There was no door chime, no sound, nothing. It was like he materialized out of nowhere.

"Jiminy Cricket, Mr. Burns, you frightened me," Lisa said, gasping.

"I always come in the front door. I have my own passkey," Bob said. "Did Josie introduce you to Pastor John and get you acclimated to everything?"

Lisa was still catching her breath. "I met the Pastor and Josie showed me a few things. She said you would finish showing me everything else," Lisa said.

Bob stood there a moment, sizing Lisa up again. He had already interviewed her and given her the job, but he liked to size a person up in the work environment.

Lisa felt uncomfortable.

"Come over here and sit down. We'll get you situated," he said.

Bob and Lisa sat at the breakfast table where just a few minutes before John had been eating breakfast. Lisa said, "I would offer you some coffee, but I'm not even sure where the coffee maker is. Would you like some juice or some water?"

Bob responded in an almost monotone voice, "The coffee maker is in the cabinet to the right side of the fridge. There is coffee in the pantry. And no, I don't need anything, but thank you."

"You're welcome." Lisa felt she needed to be careful around Mr. Burns. There was something about him. She couldn't put her finger on it.

"Let's get you logged into the house system," Bob said. He pulled a paper out of his briefcase.

"Computer, new login. Authorization: 77215 Bob Burns." The house answered. "Authorization approved. I'm ready for a new login, Bob."

"Lisa Smithy, 10457 53rd Avenue, Apartment 23B."

"Confirmed," the computer replied.

"Social Security number, 436-03-1506," Bob added.

"Confirmed," the computer replied.

"Date of birth: May 2, 1996."

"Confirmed," the computer replied.

"Initiate voice recognition sequence," Bob said.

"Ready for voice recognition sequence," the computer said. "Lisa Smithy, please state and spell your name."

Bob looked over at Lisa. She looked a little unsure. He waved his hand at her to go ahead.

"Lisa Smithy. L I S A S M I T H Y," she said.

The computer responded, "Processing."

Less than 10 seconds passed, and the computer said, "Voice recognition sequence completed. Welcome, Lisa Smithy. May I call you Lisa?

Lisa smiled, "Uh, yes, that will be fine. What shall I call you?"

"John likes to call me Freda. I will answer to the computer, or you may speak directly to the appliance or house system you are needing," the computer said.

Bob stepped in. "If it is too hot, you only have to say 'air-conditioning, please cool the room three degrees,' and it will respond."

The computer spoke, "Bob, are you asking for the room to be cooled three degrees?"

Bob answered, "No, I was just giving an example to Lisa. Go to monitor mode," Bob said.

Silence.

"When you ask the computer to go to monitor mode, it stops responding to vocal commands unless it senses you want it to respond. It is a very sophisticated system, replying not only to content but also to the emotional tone of your voice. If you have an emergency, you just say 'emergency' or tell it to call 911. If you want to make a phone call, you just ask for a phone. If you want a private call, there are handsets in every room, in the garages, and on the patio. You can also pick up a handset and talk directly to the computer.

"Outside on the perimeter of the house, there are sensors and speakers. So if you are taking John out for a walk in the garden and he falls, you can call for help from the yard. You can order a lockdown of the house by your voice and a passkey or order any door or any of the four garages open by your voice and a passkey. Your passkey is your voice and the last four digits of your Social Security number."

"Computer, go to phone synchronization," Bob commanded. Then he turned to Lisa. "Lisa, would you get your cell phone?"

Lisa got up to retrieve her cell phone from her purse. Freda responded, "Ready for phone synchronization."

"Lisa, make sure your wireless and Bluetooth apps are on," Bob instructed her.

Lisa hesitated, then looked at her phone. "Uh, both are showing on my screen, I think," Lisa said.

"That's fine. Computer, sync with Lisa's cell phone," Bob said.

"Synchronization is underway," Freda answered. "Completed. Lisa, a new app is being uploaded to your phone. Use your passkey when you are ready to activate it."

"Uh, okay. I will," Lisa answered.

"With the app, you can secure and unlock the house, open any of the garages, adjust the heat or air, turn lights on or off... everything you can do while in the house. Also, when you are ready to go shopping the computer will send a shopping list to your phone," Bob said.

Lisa sat there with her mouth ajar and her eyes wide open. She had heard about smart houses and seen them on HGTV, but she had never been in one.

Bob went on. "When the developers built the gated community, this was the demonstration house. Potential buyers were shown what could be done if they built here. At the time this house was state of the art. There are much more advanced systems now."

Bob continued. "The house has two levels, upper and lower. There are five bedrooms, two up and three down, five and a half baths. On this level, there is a formal dining room and music room, the den, breakfast nook and kitchen, a guest room and bath, and a study. Downstairs you'll find the other bedrooms and baths, an exercise room, a small second kitchen, a media room, four garages and an elevator. There is no pool, but in the back are formal gardens and a playground. Did Josie take you downstairs?"

"No," Lisa shook her head.

"Computer, open the elevator in the den."

Lisa heard the sound of an elevator rising. Then one of the bookshelf units on the wall in the den released and opened. There it was. An elevator.

Bob and Lisa stepped inside the oak-paneled elevator just as John entered the kitchen, dressed but wearing his house shoes.

He slowly inched his way across the kitchen and into the den. He backed up to his lift chair, already in the up position, and eased himself down. He reached over, found the remote and pushed the button. The chair slowly lowered and then reclined.

John was tired. He needed to rest. His eyes soon shut.

~~~~~

He almost always dreamed about Frankie. At first, he would awaken shaking and in tears. Later the dreams became a kind of comfort. She still lived in his mind and heart.

By faith, John believed she did live, in heaven with God. He had preached this all his life in hundreds of funeral sermons. When his parents died, he felt assured of their eternal security and that he would see them again. When Frankie's parents died, the same thing.

When Frankie died, for the first time in his life he doubted. She had fought bravely and suffered much in her two-year fight with pancreatic cancer. He had spent many nights at her bedside praying to God, begging God, to deliver her from this disease.

Looking back, he was very selfish. But he could not help himself. He could not imagine life without her. Over time, his confidence in the Gospel came back. Frankie was safe in heaven. He was confident of it. They would be together again.

He dreamed of her from years ago.

Frances Bullock was the only child of Charles and Lois. Her dad always wanted a boy, so he raised her like a boy and nicknamed her Frankie. It stuck.

She grew up a tomboy, excelling at sports, music, and in the classroom. A natural beauty selected most beautiful her senior year in high school, she wore little makeup. In a flash, she could go from the softball field to a beauty pageant.

She also grew up in a faith-filled home. Things of God were openly talked about and celebrated in her family, and church was a joyous part of her life. She made a profession of faith in Christ as an older child and never wavered from that commitment.

She couldn't really pinpoint when it happened, but as a young teen, she felt like she was called to be a pastor's wife. For a long time that was the only call recognized for women, except foreign missions. Though later churches started accepting young women who were called to the ministry, Frankie always said it would not have mattered. Her call was certain. She had no objection to women in ministry. She celebrated it, but her call was to be a pastor's wife.

That came in handy when John met her. He, too, had a strong sense of God's call on his life from a young age. He and his best friend, Joe Holloway, were in the Boy Scouts together. They were always serious boys. One day they were talking about the scout pledge: "On my honor, I will do my best, to do my duty to God and my country ..."

John looked at Joe and said, "I will do my duty to my God."

Joe said to John, "I will do my duty to my country."

John became a pastor, and Joe a politician.

It made a great story, one that both of them enjoyed telling for years. It didn't exactly happen that way, but it made a great story.

At six foot four, Joe was a stand-out athlete who went to the state university on a baseball scholarship. A shoulder injury ended any dream of the major leagues, so Joe headed to law school. After several years in private practice, he ran for and served six years in the state legislature, and then was elected two terms as governor. Two years into his second term, when longtime Senator Sam Beckum died, Joe did the unusual thing of appointing himself senator and resigning as governor. A year later he won a special election to his own six-year term as a United States Senator.

John attended a small Christian college, majoring in Bible with the intent to move on to seminary as soon as he graduated. Then he met this beautiful girl, Frankie. It was love at first sight. He felt called to be a preacher, she felt called to be a preacher's wife; they were the darlings of that small Christian college campus. Everyone knew John and Frankie would be successful.

They married right after college graduation.

John went on to seminary. Frankie taught high school English. After seminary, he pastored a small rural church, and they had four children. Through it all, she continued to teach.

Denominational leaders saw potential in John and encouraged him with scholarship offers to return to seminary for doctoral work. John thought differently. Instead, he went to the state university and earned a Ph.D. in Philosophy and Religion.

Then he was called as pastor of First Church in the capital city. John had preached there on a few occasions over the years, and he and Frankie felt like they would one day serve that great church. In answering the church's call John had written, "We felt the subtle squeeze of the hand of Providence the first time we walked on this campus. We joyfully accept the affirmation of God's hand in your call." It was a great match.

The church covered three city blocks and had a long, rich history. There was a large, Tudor-style parsonage in a well-established neighborhood near the church. It was no longer in the best part of town, was old and in need of repair, but John and Frankie loved it. Instead of accepting a housing allowance and purchasing their own home on the outskirts of the city, they convinced the church to go along with their plans to restore it to its 1950's glory.

Frankie completed her master's degree and was soon teaching at the local community college. Their children were growing up, they were involved in ministry and in the community, and they had many friends—it was a wonderful life.

~~~~~

"John," Bob said as he shook him by the shoulder. "John."

John opened his eyes.

"Bob, how are you today?" His voice sounded parched.

Bob picked up the water mug—it was empty—and handed it to Lisa. She hurried into the kitchen and used the ice and water dispenser on the refrigerator door to fill the mug, and returned.

Lisa held the mug as John moved the straw to his mouth.

"Thank you," he said after taking several sips.

Bob said, "I've shown Lisa all around most of the house. She is logged into the house system. I think you guys are all set."

John did not say anything.

Bob turned to Lisa. "You've got my number. If you need anything, call. Good luck."

With that Bob Burns left the way he came—out the front door. Only this time it chimed when he opened the door. "That was odd," Lisa thought.

She stood beside the recliner where John sat for a moment. He said nothing.

Finally, she said, "Okay, what would you like to do now?"

He looked at her. He looked away and shut his eyes.

Lisa had a nervous habit of twisting her hair between two fingers. She caught herself doing that, and stopped.

"I'll go make up the bed," she said. And she was off.

John thought to himself. "That's good. She didn't try and force conversation, and she didn't sit down and turn on the TV. She is task-oriented."

He checked one thing off his mental checklist. There were many more.

3

THE LIST

Day two began without incident. Lisa arrived early before John got up. When he stirred, she waited for him at his bedroom door.

"Good morning, Pastor John," she said with a cheery voice.

He did not respond. Josie said he was moody and if he didn't want to talk, not to force the issue.

Lisa had his cranberry juice already on the table and was preparing French toast. That's what was on the menu, with yogurt. She decided not to ask; she just placed it on the table before him without a word.

John said softly, "Thank you."

Lisa responded, "You're welcome."

She got her own food and sat opposite him at the table. She assumed that his late wife would have sat next to him. Yesterday for lunch and dinner she had eaten in the kitchen, but somehow she was certain he would be okay with her at the table, but not in Frankie's spot.

John thought to himself. "She is good. She can live with silence. She did not try and sit in Frankie's chair. She is very observant." He checked off another item on his mental list.

John read the paper on his iPad and ate. Lisa looked out the window at the beautiful gardens below while she ate. What a lovely house and grounds. She hoped John would want to go outside soon and walk around the garden. Maybe tomorrow she could pick some fresh flowers and have them on the table.

But then, she bet that was the kind of thing his late wife had done. She decided to ask.

"Pastor John, would you mind if I brought in some fresh flowers one morning?

Without looking up from his iPad John said, "That will be fine."

Again, he made a mental note about her. She asked first. Check another off.

As he finished eating, she got his morning meds and placed them before him and poured a fresh glass of juice.

"Are you a coffee drinker? I'll be happy to make some coffee," she said.

John cleared his throat. "I've never been a big fan of coffee. On some mornings I may ask for some. You may make some for yourself if you like," he answered.

She did love coffee, but she wondered if it was a good idea. It was just a guess, but she figured Frankie loved coffee.

John said, "My late wife loved coffee. I sort of miss the smell of coffee in the morning."

Lisa took a sip of water and smiled. She guessed the previous day sitters had come in and taken over the kitchen like it was their own and had not bothered to consider what he liked or didn't. She needed to act like a guest in this house.

John thought to himself, "She did not come in here like she owned the place. That's good." And he checked another off.

Soon she had picked out clothes for him to wear, and he proceeded to the shower while she cleaned up the kitchen. She asked the refrigerator for an inventory list and those items set to expire soon. If she didn't know better, she would have thought that Freda was happy someone finally asked.

She went through the pantry and called out things that should be on the shopping list and then she asked for the list.

A moment later her phone dinged. She opened the house app, and there it was.

"Jiminy Cricket," Lisa said out loud. She thought to herself, "This house is amazing."

John called out to her. She went into his room where he was sitting in a chair with his shoes on the floor and socks in his hand. "Can you help me?" he asked.

"Be glad to. Do you want to go somewhere?"

"We're going shopping, aren't we?" he said.

Lisa smiled. "Yes, we need to get a few things."

She finished helping him with his socks and shoes. Then, cautiously she spoke. "I need to know how to best go about this."

John explained that there was a mini-van in the first garage. The keys were on a hook just beside the door to the garages. They could ride the elevator down together. He went into detail on exactly how they would get there and back. He told her the store would have a scooter chair he could use to get around.

Lisa already knew most of these details. Josie or Mr. Burns had gone over it all. She had been to this store before. What she really wanted to know was what happened when they got there. Would she have to follow him around, or would he follow her around, or would he go off on his own while she went down the list? Would she have to find him?

John sensed her uneasiness. "Don't worry," he said. "I can keep myself occupied while you get whatever is needed. I won't leave the store."

Lisa laughed softly. "Well, you're an adult. You can go where you want," she said.

Check off another one, John thought. She wasn't going to treat him like an invalid child.

"Let me sit here and rest a few moments; then I'll be ready to go."

About 30 minutes later they were in the mini-van backing out of the garage. Lisa asked, "How do I get the garage to shut?"

John said, "Just tell it to and give your passkey."

Lisa's mind raced, "Passkey. Mr. Burns told me about the passkey thing. What was it?"

"I'm sorry Pastor John, what was the passkey thing?" she finally had to ask.

"It's your voice, plus...

"...the last four digits of your Social Security number," she said with him, now remembering.

"Do I roll down the window and say it to the house?" she asked.

John pointed to a device that looked sort of like a garage door opener that was hanging on the driver side sunshade. It had a little blinking LED light. "Just talk," he said.

Lisa said tentatively, "Shut the garage door, 1506."

The garage door shut.

Lisa smiled, feeling rather proud of herself.

"Now, secure the house," John said.

She hesitated.

"Just say it," he encouraged her.

"Secure the house, 1506."

Freda's voice came out of the little box with the blinking light. "The house is secure."

"Jiminy Cricket!" Lisa said with amazement.

John checked off another one on his list. *She isn't afraid to ask when she doesn't know something.*

Shopping went without incident. As they left, John suggested they get a *Subway* sandwich and save Lisa the trouble of preparing lunch. Lisa went through the drive-through, using the debit card Mr. Burns had given her for all job-related expenses, being sure to save the receipt.

Back at the house, they ate their sandwiches quietly at the table. Afterward, John settled into his recliner, and she put away the groceries and household supplies. After that, she made his bed and straightened his bathroom. John was asleep as she curled into a chair in the den and began reading a book.

~~~~~

John was in the main conference room at the church. The Board was meeting. Attendance had dropped precipitously. Giving was dramatically down. People were starting to point fingers and place blame. These board members were hearing it.

There were two staff vacancies and the motion on the floor was not only to leave them vacant but also to eliminate a third staff position. The idea of letting someone go made John ill.

John stood before his Board. He looked around the room at a group of men and women who had followed his leadership and supported him in nearly everything he sought to do at First Church. These were good men and women who cared about this church and the work of the Kingdom.

It had all started last year when the Board recommended changes to their by-laws. The new language stated that First Church believes the Scriptures teach that marriage is an exclusive relationship between a man and a woman.

The Supreme Court had issued a decision a few months earlier that had made same-sex marriage legal in all 50 states. It left churches that believed in traditional marriage in danger of being sued unless they took specific action related to their governing documents.

Ironically, churches that would accept the new concept as marriage between anyone did not have to do anything. But churches that held to traditional marriage as handed down through the ages had to adopt new language stating so.

Three kinds of churches were emerging: those who would not accept homosexuality no matter what; those whose doors were open to homosexuals but would not support gay marriage; and those who accepted it all.

Churches in the third category put up banners celebrating their openness. Churches in the second category were busy changing their governing documents while trying to show openness to all people. Those in the first category just spit out their dogma. It was the first and last groups that were getting all the press. Churches like First Church were quietly trying to stay true to their confession while holding on to their membership.

A small but vocal group left First Church because they thought the church was taking the wrong steps. They went to an accepting church. John worked hard to say to each family that even though they disagreed, they remained brothers and sisters in Christ. For the most part, he was successful.

Another vocal group left because they thought Pastor John was too weak on the subject. They left kicking the dust off their feet. John tried to make the parting peaceful but was largely unsuccessful.

The last group left quietly but in large numbers. They were tired of the debate. They just wanted to worship Jesus without all the culture war stuff. NorthPointe Community Church, a non-denominational church just North of the loop, did not seem to have a discussion like this.

What they failed to realize was that NorthPointe indeed had such a discussion, but it was held among a small select group of elders who held total power over the church. They changed their bylaws to reflect the same policy First Church had adopted without the church ever having to discuss it or vote on it.

The consequences for a church with a congregational-type polity—where everything was subject to discussion and debate before the church in General Session—were nearly devastating. Though it was of no comfort, John realized the same thing was happening to churches like his all across the country.

Being a big downtown church that was televised, and the fact that John had been president of the national denominations just a few years ago, the whole state took note of the coming congregational vote on marriage. Protestors showed up two weeks prior. John and others took water out to them and invited them to worship if they would agree to not disrupt the service. Some took him up, but as soon as he got up to preach, they started chanting and marching around the sanctuary. They cut off the broadcast, but not quickly enough. The entire state saw one of his "loving" members, red in the face with anger, jump up and rip a sign from a protestor's hands. It ended up on *YouTube* and went viral.

The next week, the church, in addition to the water, rented tents for the protestors to get a break from the hot sun. Again, John invited them in to worship under the same conditions. The same thing happened, only this time they were already broadcasting a previously recorded service.

John told the protestors that a Sunday School class had made lunch for them and invited them all in to eat, even the ones who had disrupted the service.

They came. That ended up being a positive experience. On the night of the vote, the protestors decided to picket another church.

The vote was, as John expected, to accept the new bylaws language. But the die was cast.

A little more than a year later First Church was running 30% fewer in worship, and they were over a quarter of a million dollars behind budget.

John told the Board that he and Frankie had discussed and prayed about it. He was willing to accept a 20% cut in pay. By not filling the other positions he felt they would not have to cut any other staff.

Many of the Board members protested. John hoped they would step up to the plate and commit the needed extra funds to the budget that night. A few did, but not enough.

John was still confident the situation could be turned around. Then his single largest contributor invited him to lunch the next day.

The timing was not good, he admitted, but he and his wife had decided they were leaving First Church. They were going to an accepting church. He would, however, complete his pledge for the year. He said to John, "Pastor, it's not personal."

~~~~~

John said aloud, "It's not personal."

Lisa lowered her book. "I beg your pardon?"

John's open eyes focused on another time and place. Lisa had noticed before the deep wrinkles etched into the corners of his eyes and mouth, but today she realized they represented the personal suffering he had known. But his clear blue eyes danced with a melody of compassion. His hair was still dark, but it was thinning in the back, noticeably now.

John blinked and cleared his throat. He was back.

"May I have some water please?" he asked.

Lisa was up immediately holding the straw to his lips.

"You said something, Pastor. I didn't understand what you said," she replied.

John drank some more water. Then he pushed himself up in his chair.

"I said it's not personal."

Lisa put the water mug down and took a tissue to his lips. She waited a moment.

"Okay," she said, "whatever it is, it's not personal."

He looked at her and suddenly remembered. "Margaret. That was your mother, right?"

Lisa smiled. "Yes sir. She was a member of your congregation," she said.

He raised his finger. "I remember when you were born," he added.

"Yes sir. She told me you came by and prayed a blessing on me. She also told me how you reached out to my father. Mother always spoke highly of you," she commented.

John closed his eyes. How many times did he stand in the maternity suite of the hospital, place one hand on a baby and one hand on the mother and pray, "Dear Father, your Son always welcomed the little children to come unto Him. He surely welcomes little Lisa—or Jack, or Sue, or whatever the name was—just as this family welcomes her. May you bless them with all the happiness that family can bring, all the wisdom these parents will need, and in your timing welcome this child into your kingdom."

He had done that hundreds of times. It never got old.

"Your family left. Where did you go?" he asked.

"Pastor John," Lisa sighed. "It's not a particularly happy story. Well, it's my story and I'm not an unhappy person, but things were not easy," she said.

John wondered. "Will she trust me with her story?"

She continued. "Let me just say that my father's work sent us to Oregon when I was seven, and his love for the bottle destroyed his marriage. I cannot blame my father for my troubles. Mr. Burns knows all about my drug issues and rehab. I can't blame my father, but he broke my mother's heart. She died when I was 19."

"But God found me and helped me find myself. God put me back together."

She paused. "Oh heck, I guess if I'm going to get fired you might as well know it all. I got pregnant and had an abortion."

A single tear ran down her right cheek.

"I got a bottle of booze that night, went back to my apartment to get drunk. And I did. It sounds crazy, but I came to in the middle of the night, and Jesus was sitting in my room watching me. When I finally got up around noon that next day, I had the strange sensation that He had been with me all night. That's when I got cleaned up, and I've been clean ever since."

Her eyes swam with tears.

"You're not going to be fired," John said with a breaking voice.

He wished Frankie was here. Frankie would take her up in her arms and love on her like she was her own child. All Pastor John could do was wipe his eyes and reach out and pat Lisa's hand.

Perhaps he had found her.

4

THE QUESTIONS

The next morning John was a little late getting up. Lisa had fresh flowers from the garden on the table, and he could smell a pot of coffee. She had her hair down this morning for a change.

John shuffled into the room to Lisa's cheery "Good morning pastor."

He just nodded at her.

"Maybe he's just not a morning person," she thought to herself.

Today's breakfast was pancakes, turkey bacon, and fresh fruit. She busied herself getting it ready. John's juice was on the table.

As he sat down, he said, "The coffee smells good. I think I'll have a cup with my breakfast if it's not too much trouble."

"No trouble at all," Lisa responded. "Do you like it black?"

"No, I like cream and sugar—or that sweetener they tell me to use. The flowers are nice," he added.

Lisa smiled.

As they ate together, Lisa asked, "I'm here six days a week. But every third weekend I get an extra day off, and I don't come on Sundays at all. May I ask who helps you then?"

"Well," John said, "on Sundays and on your extra day, either Marilyn Holloway, Senator Joe Holloway's widow, comes, or Mike Summers and his wife, Jane. Mike was my associate at First Church. If neither of them can make it, then I'm stuck with Bob Burns.

Lisa thought, "I want to know more about that guy."

John thought, "I'm not ready to tell you about Bob Burns, yet."

He continued, "Occasionally my daughter Jennifer from Texas or my daughter-in-law Cheryl from Florida comes to spend a weekend with me. They'll often bring grandchildren with them. And twice a year my daughter Rachel will have some time off and will fly in from Africa."

"Oh, I didn't realize one of your daughters lived in Africa," she said.

"Yes, she is a director with *Compassion International* helping the children of Sudan."

She hadn't always been in Africa. Appointed by the denominational mission board to serve in Haiti, Rachel had served there about seven years.

He remembered the conversation. Home for a visit, Rachel was frustrated with the mission board.

"Dad, all they want me to do is serve as an in-country travel agent, making arrangements for oversized mission groups."

John explained to her how when churches do hands-on missions they give more to missions. It was great pubic relations.

"I'm not there to do public relations for the denomination," she said. "That's not what God has called me to do. Every time a group arrives they come off the buses with their phones and cameras flashing. They fawn over the children like they are the most precious things on earth and then they leave. They don't understand why it's not a good thing to peel off dollars to give to the people. They leave with smug self-satisfaction like they have done something so worthwhile that it will last them the rest of their lives. Frankly, Dad, they do as much harm as they do good."

Shortly after that she resigned her appointment with the Mission Board and accepted a position with *Compassion International* in sub-Sahara Africa. John's best friend, Senator Joe Holloway, was on the board of Compassion and had helped make this happen. Once in Africa she got to help children and did not have to host mission teams. She also was able to share a credible witness with some very secular *UNICEF* relief workers they partnered with. She quickly advanced to a director's position.

"I can't wait to meet her. When is she due stateside again?" Lisa asked.

"Sometime this summer," John answered.

"Don't you have two sons, also?" Lisa asked.

Pastor John took a sip of his coffee. "Ahh, this coffee is just right, Lisa," he said. He took another sip.

Lisa decided he wasn't going to answer when he finally said, "Yes. Ben lives in California. Frank is in Florida. Both are busy with work. Neither has come since their mother's death."

Lisa thought to herself, "That's been three years. He hasn't seen his sons in three years."

As if he knew what she was thinking, he added, "I have been to see them, both of them, on many occasions. Before this stroke, I was free to travel, and I did. But they have not been here." Then he added, "I've not seen either of them since before my stroke."

Lisa thought he was despondent when he said that. An untold sadness hovered over this family.

John was not ready to tell her everything. There was still one more test she needed to pass. Today was exam day.

Lisa realized she might have asked too much. She really wanted to know about his children and grandchildren. There were photos all over the house, but there was no evidence that they visited very often. And Bob Burns, well, he was creepy, and she really wanted to know more about him.

But, it was none of her business. He would tell her if he wanted to.

Since the first day, she felt like he was testing her, like he had some kind of checklist he was going down. She felt like yesterday had been an essential part of that process. She felt like today would be, also.

"Lisa, after I've showered and rested a bit, let's talk some," John said.

"Okay, Pastor," she said.

Yep, she was right. Today the finals would begin.

After John's shower, he got in his recliner and rested. Lisa cleaned up the kitchen and started washing clothes. After a while, she carried a hamper with clothes fresh from the dryer into the den. She began folding them.

John was awake. "From our talk yesterday I gather you are a believer," he said.

"Yes," she responded. "I would never have made it if it weren't for my faith in God."

"Do you go to church?" he asked.

"NorthPoint Church," she answered.

"Did you go to church in Oregon?"

"You know, crazy as it might sound, I never stopped going to church, not even when I was doing drugs. I even helped in the children's Sunday School."

She went on. "When you're doing drugs, you fool yourself into thinking that nobody notices. But people do. They just don't know how to respond to you, and if they do say anything you've always got an excuse," she said.

"What brought you back here from out west?" he continued.

"Well," she said as she folded towels, "after I went through rehab my grandmother got really sick. My mother was gone, and I didn't have much of a relationship with my father, so I came to the state to take care of her. She died about a year later, I moved to the city, and I've been helping elderly people ever since."

"Do you ever blame God?" he asked.

"Blame God for what?" she answered as she folded one of his t-shirts.

"For your mother's death? For your father's alcoholism? For your own drug problems? For the bad decision you made in life?"

"Listen, Pastor, one of the things you have to learn if you are a drug addict and if you are going to live clean is that you can't blame anyone else for your problems. You have to take responsibility for your own life," she answered emphatically.

"But you blame your father for your mother's death."

Lisa was taken back by that. She felt anger stir within her, anger she had long tried to do away with.

She looked at him. "You're good, Pastor John. It took my therapist four months to make me realize that. I haven't been here four days."

John pushed. "Then it's true, you blame your father."

"Yes," Lisa popped a towel and quickly folded it and added it to the stack. "I blame him because he broke her heart."

She grabbed another towel. "My mother was an angel, a saint. She was trusting, way too trusting. She believed up until he ran off with another woman that she was going to be able to make everything work, that they would grow old together and that I would get married and bring her grandchildren. She was wrong on every count. She never got over it."

"So you do blame your father for your troubles," he said.

"No, I don't," she insisted.

"But you do think he is responsible for your mother's death, and that is what sent you spiraling out of control," John continued to push.

"I was already out of control," Lisa almost shouted. "Okay!"

She paused.

"My mother was clueless. All she could do was clean up the mess he made of everything. She didn't have time to stay on top of what I was doing."

"I see now. You really blame your mother," John said.

"No, I don't blame her. I don't blame him. I am responsible for the decisions I made," she said firmly.

"So you blame God," he said forcefully.

She looked at him with tears in her eyes.

"Why are you doing this? Why are you asking all these questions?" she wanted to know.

"Because I want to know if you blame God. You know God has a lot to answer for," he responded.

"What?" she asked, puzzled. She had never heard talk like this, especially from a pastor.

"He does," John pushed on. "God has a lot to answer for. Like the Christmas Eve I got this phone call. This man whose wife had left him and abandoned her two little boys called me just before midnight. All he said was 'Pastor, pray that God will forgive me,' and he hung up. I looked at the caller I.D. and I knew who he was. I called the sheriff, and he told me they had already had a call from this guy and that they were on their way to his house. He asked me to come, too."

"You won't believe what we found. That man had put his boys in bed together on Christmas Eve, and then after they were asleep, he went into the room and shot both of them in the head. Then he called the sheriff and told them what he had done. He waited about ten minutes; then he called me. After that, he put the gun in his mouth and pulled the trigger. That is what the Sheriff found when they arrived.

"Because I was the last person to talk to him alive, they wanted to know whatever I knew. All I knew was that the man had been diagnosed with prostate cancer. It was treatable, but he didn't figure he would live to see the boys raised. You know why he did it? He hated his wife so much he didn't want her to get them."

Lisa looked at Pastor John's eyes as he told the story. She could hardly believe what she was hearing. "Pastor, that is horrible, just horrible."

"Where was God, Lisa? Where was God? There were Christmas presents under the tree and two brand new bicycles in the garage. Why didn't God stop that from happening? What had those two boys done to deserve this?" he asked.

"Pastor, I don't know. I don't know where God was." She put her face down on the towel she was holding.

"I did a triple funeral—three caskets; one large one and two small ones, in a row—the day after Christmas."

Lisa softly cried into the towel.

"Or these two men I knew, a father and his adult son. They came out of the woods after deer hunting. They were on a remote gravel road, had the heater on full blast and country music blaring from the radio. They did not hear or see the train that was barreling down full speed. There was no barrier or warning lights at the crossing. They never knew what hit them."

"That was on Christmas Eve, too, Lisa. I got the call just after dark. There was one grieving woman who lost her husband and her son, and another grieving woman who lost her husband and was left with an infant.

"Where was God, Lisa? Where was God when that train crushed their pickup truck? WHERE WAS GOD!" John said forcefully.

Lisa cried out, "Stop it, Pastor John. Stop it. Just stop it!"

"You don't know, do you?" he asked after a moment. "But you told me you believe in God. You told me Jesus came and sat with you all night. You told me he changed your life and because of Him you got cleaned up, and you stay clean. It is easy to believe in God when good things happen to you, but what about senseless, unfair things like this? What about those two boys? What about those two men?

"What about my wife?" he demanded.

Lisa got up and ran from the room.

John, shaking, leaned back in his recliner. His heart was beating irregularly, and he had a hard time getting his breath. He closed his eyes and focused on breathing.

Then he prayed, "Dear God, I want her to be the one. I want her to have the faith. Give her strength. Speak to her, Lord. Don't let her run out like the others. I want to make things right, but I need someone's help, someone I can trust, someone who really believes. Help her Lord. Help her to forgive me."

John sat in his chair, his heart pounding and tears running down his cheeks.

Lisa ran out the kitchen door and down the side of the house to the back. She ran down the path into the garden to a bench under the outspread arms of a live oak. She sat and wept. Why was he doing this? Why? She knew it was some kind of test; she just didn't know why.

Then she understood. Lisa fell to her knees. The wind tossed her auburn hair to and fro. She prayed for John. "Dear God, Pastor John is hurting. This is why you have brought me here. Show me how to help him. Tell me what to say to him. Help me have the faith."

Exhausted, John was soon asleep.

He dreamed of Frankie.

~~~~~

Lisa gently woke him up.

"Pastor John," she said softly as she squeezed his hand. "I've got your lunch ready."

John came back to the present. He looked up at her. She had her hair pulled back into a ponytail again. She smiled a sweet, loving smile. She was radiant.

"I've got chicken salad for us," she said, and handed him the remote for his lift chair, moving his walker into position for him.

John made his way to the bathroom. When he returned, lunch was on the table along with the fresh-cut flowers from this morning. He sat down.

Lisa said, "Pastor, we have failed to do this at our meals. Would you say a blessing for us?"

John said, "Yes. I would love to."

They bowed their heads, and John prayed a short but sincere blessing. Then they began to eat in silence.

There was a soft rumble of thunder. The sky darkened outside. It started to rain, a spring thundershower.

After a while, Lisa spoke. "Pastor, I know where God was. I know where He was each time. I know where He was when your sweet wife died. He was right there with you, just like He was that night with me, only when He was with you, He wept."

John looked up. He had found her.

5

THE PHONE CALL

Frankie dismissed the class, her last of the day. Put away her lecture notes, check a few emails, and she could get home early and work the flowerbed to the side of the patio.

Out in the hall, she saw John talking to a student. It made her smile.

"Hi there," Frankie said.

"Hi, honey." He looked at her and smiled. After all these years, she was as beautiful as when they first met in college, only now she kept her blond hair cut short. Truthfully, they just enjoyed seeing each other.

"Caleb was just telling me about his scholarship to State."

"I know. Isn't it exciting? Caleb is very deserving," Frankie said.

"Thank you, Mrs. Grant," the young man said. "I am really excited, and I appreciate all your help. But please excuse me, I've got to get to work."

"You run along. Say hi to your mom for us," John said.

"I will," Caleb said as he hurried away.

Frankie watched him. "I'm so happy for him. This scholarship is his ticket to wonderful things." She turned toward

John and took his arm. "Speaking of wonderful things, I am certainly surprised to see you out here at this time of day. Don't you have hospital visits to make?"

"Yes, but they are not going anywhere. This can't wait. I had a phone call a little while ago, and I had to come tell you about it," John said, his eyebrows raised.

"Oh, from whom?" Frankie asked.

"Well," John looked up and then down the crowded hallway. A girl from the church saw them and came running up.

"That's Carrie," Frankie whispered into his ear. They always helped each other with names because they knew so many people from having lived intensely public lives. It was hard to keep the names straight. John would quip, "We know more people than we know."

"Carrie," Pastor John said just as she came up.

She gave them both hugs while breathlessly exclaiming, "I'm so happy to see you. I'm going to be a camp counselor this summer. I got accepted."

Carrie was a blast of sunshine—bright, beautiful eyes, a kind heart, and an unquenchable spirit. She was just like her mother.

John and Frankie had known her family since before Carrie was born. She had grown up in the church, been baptized by John—done all the things she was supposed to do in a life that was filled with every opportunity, with little adversity, and with loving family and friends pointing her toward helping others.

Carrie and her father had been part of a mission team First Church sent to Mexico the year before. She loved it, as

John knew she would. John had recently completed a recommendation for her to a children's summer camp.

"I'm so excited about this summer," she said.

"Carrie, that's wonderful," Frankie said, giving her another hug around the neck.

"We are proud of you, Carrie," John added.

She carried her sunshine on down the hall while John leaned over to Frankie and whispered, "We need somewhere private to talk about this."

"Okay. How about an English instructor's office?" Frankie winked.

On the way to her office, they talked to at least a half a dozen people.

Finally, Frankie shut the door and sat behind her desk while John settled in the chair next to the desk, the one where students would sit to make their excuses as to why a project was not finished on time.

"Joe called," he said.

Senator Joe Holloway was John's best friend from childhood.

"What did he want?" Frankie wanted to know. Joe did not call often, but when he did something fun usually followed.

"He had a proposition, one that is really interesting."

"Okay, what did he say?"

"You won't believe this. He wants to nominate me Chaplain of the United States Senate," John said.

The words just hung in the air.

Frankie turned her head to the side and stared off somewhere, the sure sign that her mind was racing now with all the questions and ramifications of such a proposal.

"Chaplain of the Senate? John... I don't know where to begin... would you even be interested in that?"

"A couple of years ago, no way. But now, well, think about this with me. You know we had that analysis run of our church annuity, and we should have been contributing more to it all along. We helped Frank and Jennifer with their problems, nearly depleting our savings. We've always lived in a parsonage. We've never owned our own home, so we have no equity built up. This position will nearly double my salary. In five years I will qualify for a full Federal pension on top of our retirements. We could save enough for a down payment on a house."

"Honey," Frankie asked. "Is money the only reason you would consider this?"

"Of course not. I would, I mean, we would have the opportunity to minister to one hundred Senators, their staffs and the employees of the Senate. Joe and Marilyn are in Washington. They are close friends with the Vice President of the United States. It is a level of influence, of ministry, we never dreamed possible."

"But honey," Frankie objected. "We've been here a long time. All of our friends are here. What about our children and grandchildren?"

"All of our kids and their families live out of state or out of the country, Frankie. We don't see any of them very often. We might even see them more often because they would get to go to Washington D.C."

"But where would we live?" she asked. "The cost of living in D.C. is really high."

"Yes it is, but Joe said he could help us out there. Darling, five years at that salary and gaining that extra retirement, that could make a huge difference in how we live the rest of our lives."

Frankie sat back and looked at her husband. "John, all you keep talking about is the money. This isn't like you."

He sat back in his chair. "No, I guess it's not. But things have changed."

"What has changed?" she asked.

"Well, church has changed. We have been serving a local church, well, since we were kids ..."

"With kids!" she added.

"Yes," he smiled. "And I wouldn't trade a minute of it for anything else."

"But ...?" she asked.

"But, this is such a great opportunity. I would be responsible for the opening prayers of the Senate. These are written prayers, mini-sermons each one. They could even be published later."

"Like the prayers of Peter Marshall?"

"Or Robert James Smith!" John added. Smith was the current Senate Chaplain.

"Has something happened to him?"

"Joe says he just announced his retirement to take effect at the summer recess." John leaned forward. "He's been in that position seven years, and you know the impact he has had."

Frankie leaned forward. "I also know how the press has treated him. Sometimes it was awful, John."

"Yes, but that was more because of the denominational wars. He needed to respond to some of that garbage, just as I did, and he did so with integrity. That's all over now."

"Do you think so, honey?" Frankie questioned.

"Yes, I do. I think from this position we can be part of the healing process. I could arrange for meetings pulling in faith leaders from around the country. We could entertain them, help mend the torn spots from years of fighting. We could help restore the witness of the church.

"And that's not all," John continued. "We could also organize discipleship groups for men and women, senators, staffers, employees. It will be like having a congregation of over a thousand people, except they don't meet on Sundays. And guess what honey, we would have weekends," John said with a sparkle in his eyes.

Frankie sat back in her chair and looked at him. "Well, we wouldn't know what to do with them," she responded.

"We could figure it out!" he added.

~~~~~

"What is it you're going to figure out, Pastor?" Lisa said.

John realized he had been dreaming again, reliving the past and talking out loud. He stirred in his recliner a bit, smacking his dried lips. Lisa responded by picking up the water mug at his side and shoving the straw at his chin. John sat forward a bit, grabbed the straw with his hand and directed it to his lips. He closed around it and drew in the cold, refreshing liquid.

He choked just a bit, coughed a few times. Lisa was quick with a tissue, wiping his mouth. He raised his finger. He wanted more water. Lisa was right there with the straw. This time he didn't choke. He leaned back into the recliner.

Lisa was not going to let it go.

"Okay Pastor, what is it you and Frankie were going to figure out?"

John stared off into the memories of long ago. Lisa had only been sitting with him a few weeks, but she knew him by now.

She just waited. If he wanted to tell her, he would.

The clock on the mantel, a gift from the men's fellowship at First Church, ticked.

John stared.

Lisa waited.

"We were going to figure out what people do with weekends," he said.

"Oh, Pastor John. That is easy. We go to church."

"Not everybody does," John responded.

"People like us do. We always have. We go to church."

"Well, when we went to Washington D.C., we suddenly had options on the weekend."

"Now wait a minute, Pastor John, you went to Washington D.C.?"

"Yes, we did, Frankie and I."

"You mean for a visit?"

"No, we went there to live, but we didn't stay for long."

"Now Pastor John, you were the pastor of the big church downtown. My mother attended there at one time."

"I know. I remember your mother." He pointed a finger at her. "I remember when you were born. We have talked about this before."

"Yes, yes, but we moved when I was really young. I always understood that you retired from being the pastor of that big church when your wife got ill?"

John looked at her. She doesn't know. And why should she? His history in D.C. is a very short footnote. You get recognized and remembered for being the first at something. Everyone forgets about you when you're the last at something.

"I resigned as pastor of First Church to become the chaplain of the United States Senate," he told her. "I resigned from that position seven months later. Frankie died three years after that. I've been by myself ever since."

"You were the chaplain of the Senate?" Lisa was puzzled. "I didn't think they had chaplains in Congress."

"Not anymore they don't. I was the last one."

6

THE STUDY

John fumbled for the remote control for his lift chair, the lonely throne from which he presided over what remained—memories good that he cherished and memories bad he could not avoid.

"Are we going somewhere?" Lisa asked.

"Yes," John answered as the recliner slowly jerked its way forward from the leaned back position to the sliding out position. "Best get my walker ready," he said.

Lisa jumped up and pulled his walker over and positioned it in front of the rising chair. John's feet reached the floor. He fumbled with the remote until he found the stop button. Then he replaced the remote on the table where everything he needed during the course of the day was arranged —the computer/telephone handset, a favorite picture of him and Frankie taken one year at the church's annual Christmas celebration, *Vicks Vapor Rub*, *Chap Stick*, *Kleenex*, nail clippers, a penknife, his favorite Bible and his iPad.

All of that well summed up his life now.

"You've been coming to help me now for how long, a month?" he joked.

"Just a few weeks," she replied. "But who's counting?"

"I am," he said with a smile. "You've not been in the study with me, have you?"

Lisa thought for a moment. "No, I don't think so. But you and Frankie have a big ol' house. There are plenty of places I haven't been."

"It's not our house," John said. "Frankie and I never owned a house."

"Oh. I just assumed..."

John interrupted her. "Be careful what you assume Lisa. You'll make an ass out of you and me."

"Pastor John! What is that?"

"Think about the word assume—a s s u m e—ass out of you and me. That's what happens when you assume too much."

Lisa laughed. She had never heard that before. "Okay Pastor. Now, where are we going?"

"Just down the hall here," he said.

John slowly led her down the hallway off the den toward the east side of the house. The master suite, the master bath, and the laundry room were all on the other side of the kitchen on the west side of the house. To the front of the house, there was a formal dining room, an entrance hall with stairs going to the lower level and a music room with a grand piano.

"I just assumed—oops, there I go again. I thought you and Frankie must have raised your family here."

"No." Pastor John said. "Our children have only ever visited here, and not often. We came to live here after we returned from Washington."

John stopped outside the first door down the hallway. He pointed to a door down the hall on the opposite side. "That's the guest room and bath. The Vice President of the United States and his wife stayed there. If you ever need to spend the night here, that is where you can stay."

Lisa's mouth dropped open. "The Vice President stayed there? You mean James Carey has stayed there?"

"No, Jim Simpson and his wife stayed there. He was the VP for President Tate, the previous administration."

"Oh," Lisa said. "Is he still around?"

"As far as I know," John answered.

He opened the study door. The light automatically came on. It was cold.

"Freda, what is the temperature in the study?" he asked.

Freda's voice answered, "Sixty-six degrees."

"Please warm the room to seventy-four degrees," John requested.

Unseen and almost unheard motors started moving air in the room. It would take only minutes.

Also unseen and unheard, a voice-activated microphone went live.

Lisa remained in the hall looking toward the door of the bedroom where the Vice President had slept, and where Pastor John said she could sleep if she needed to.

"You were friends with the Vice President?" she asked.

John stopped and looked back at her. "We were never friends."

"But he stayed here?" she asked as she entered the study and looked around.

"We had..." John paused to think carefully about his next words. They were in the house. "We had a working relationship," he said carefully.

"Okay, let me get this straight." Lisa started walking around the oak-paneled study. In front of the fireplace on an elegant wood parquet floor, lay a beautiful exotic rug. Across the room stood a stately, executive desk. The fifteen-foot ceiling allowed two levels of book shelves, with a rolling ladder on a track for gaining access to the upper level of books. The walls were covered with degrees, awards, and photos of Pastor John, Frankie, their children, and some pretty famous people.

"You and Frankie never owned a home. You came to live here after you served as the chaplain of the United State Senate, for how long?"

"Seven months."

"Seven months. Then you came to live in this house, but you don't own it." She turned to face him. "So, whose house is it?"

"Someone let us live in this house," John responded.

Lisa stared at him, waiting for him to say more.

John said, "I'm not going to tell you who."

She looked surprised. "Is it a secret, national security and all of that?"

"No," John answered. "It's just not any of your business. Now, look over here, this is a picture of Frankie and me, along with my best friend, the late Senator Joe Holloway and his wife, and the Vice President. This was the day my appointment as Chaplain of the Senate was announced."

John turned to look at Lisa, but she wasn't looking at the photo he was showing her. She was walking around the room looking at all the other mementos and photos—a lifetime of serving as a pastor and community leader.

She turned to face him. "So, this was the Vice President's house." She said it like she had figured it out.

"No, he was from Georgia, not here. This was never his house," John answered.

"So that short creepy guy who gives me my check, Bob what's his name. This is his house?" Lisa guessed.

"No. Bob Burns is an accountant and advises me concerning my affairs. You can stop asking or trying to guess, Lisa. I'm not going to tell you." John said with finality.

She stuck out her lip like a pouting child.

John stumbled slightly.

"Please," he said. "Help me sit down. I'm feeling tired."

Lisa hurried to his side and helped him around the desk to the overstuffed leather chair. John slowly backed up to the chair. Lisa stood to the side where she could offer him assistance and keep the chair from rolling backward.

John sat down with a huff. He tired so quickly.

"Just let me rest for a few minutes," he said softly with hardly a breath. "You can look around." His eyes shut.

On the wall behind the desk hung diplomas. There was a Bachelor of Arts from a Christian college, a seminary Master of Divinity degree, and a Doctor of Philosophy degree from the state university. There were photos of him in cap and gown with Frankie by his side, one for all three degrees. His children were in the picture from when he got his Ph.D.

There was a photo of him and Frankie at their wedding. They were so young. She was beautiful. They looked so in love. There was a photo of all four children, like stair steps, sitting on a bench at a photographer's studio; hair neatly combed and brushed; the boys in ties, the girls in cute dresses with ribbons. The younger girl, Jennifer, was showing a missing-tooth grin. The youngest boy, Ben, looked distracted, lost, like he didn't want to be there.

"There's a lifetime on these walls," Lisa said out loud to no one as she walked around.

~~~~~

John was back in his study at the church, arguing with Ben, again. They argued a lot.

Soon after his college graduation, Ben had informed his parents that he was gay. From the beginning, John and Frankie tried to convince him he was wrong. They tried to bargain with him, to talk him out of it. He was just confused, they told him. Now he was planning to quit his job and move out west with his newest partner.

Ben was adamant. He handed them a booklet he had been given by a counselor at the state university. It was for religious parents of gay students. The intent was to explain to parents what it meant when their son or daughter discovered they were gay and how they must accept it.

"I've seen this booklet before," John said. "You're not the first student I've known who has been given one of these."

"I guess you also know about the book they gave me on how to accept that you are gay. I read it, and Dad, it's the first time in my life that everything made sense," Ben replied.

"I have a copy of that book, too, Ben. It also has a chapter about how to convert your family. Your mother and I see what you are doing, and it won't work. Listen Ben, we love you; your whole family does. And we want what is best for you. From a biblical perspective, this is very simple."

Ben interrupted. "'The Bible says'—I knew that's what you would say, Dad. I knew you wouldn't understand. All you can do is spit out the church's line on sexuality."

"You're partially right, Ben, I don't understand. But I love you, and I'm committed to a biblical world-view because of what I have come to believe about the Word of God, not because of what anyone else says."

"But you know what, Dad? Many Christians don't agree with you. And some of them are in your own denomination."

Ben was correct about that. There was an era known as the "Denominational Wars" when many issues, such as human sexuality, caused deep rifts between churches, pastors, and people. Tired of the infighting, many fled to non-denominational churches. This resulted in an ugly war of words between independent and denominational ministers. Some people quit church altogether. Churches everywhere declined.

People who opposed religion in the public arena took advantage of the situation. Churches like First Church, with over 200 years of ministry, were marginalized. It was a dark, painful period. And in the middle of it all came Ben and his situation.

Night after night John and Frankie were on their knees praying that God would change Ben's heart. Frankie spent hours on the phone with him, gently trying to persuade him that what he thought was true, was really something else. Eventually Ben stopped accepting her calls.

John and Frankie had watched other families deal with this. Most ended up delivering an ultimatum, hoping and praying their child would choose a relationship with them rather than the gay lifestyle. Most were disappointed. In many instances, all contact with their child was severed. In one situation where John was deeply involved, the young man committed suicide. The family felt that staying true to their faith meant shunning their wayward child. Isolated and alone, he chose that path to end his pain.

John and Frankie thought differently. The heart of the Gospel is love. They would not, could not allow this sin or any sinfulness to destroy their relationship with their son. They asked, "What would Jesus do?" The answer they found was to love him unconditionally. Loving their son did not mean they accepted his world-view. Loving their son did not mean they endorsed his lifestyle. Loving their son was what God intended them to do when Ben was entrusted to them. It is what Jesus would do, even while refusing to accept his gay identity.

Finally, one night, Frankie said they would have to love Ben as he was and love whomever he was with, unconditionally, while not condoning immoral behavior. It was a fine line, but they would have to try and walk it. John agreed. Two of the other children also agreed, but not Jennifer.

According to Jennifer's husband, James Pollock, Ben was in sin. This was wrong, and if John and Frankie were going to allow Ben and his lovers into the house, then he, his wife and their two children would not be coming.

Like the church and the denomination, now his family was splintering.

Ben accused John of siding with Jennifer's husband and not accepting him or his partner. He felt like everyone would be better off if he just left the state and got far away.

John begged Ben not to leave. No matter what, he insisted, he and Frankie loved him. John also acknowledged it would not be easy and asked Ben to be patient.

Ben left the office that day and went to see his mother. She gave him some money, as John knew she would. Ben didn't return—not for Christmas, for other holidays, for birthdays, not for anything—until just before his mother died.

John and Frankie flew out west to see him, several times. On one visit, they met Robert Schroeder, his latest partner. They both instantly liked Robert and realized he was good for Ben. John and Robert had a hard conversation about their different views of life. In the end, they agreed to disagree but to try and love one another.

Since this was the life Ben chose, they hoped he would stay with Robert instead of a revolving door of relationships. They prayed he would fall under the conviction of the Spirit. They also prayed that he would be safe and that there could be some sort of reconciliation. On their last visit out west, Robert agreed to help them. He would talk to Ben.

Then news came that James Pollock, Jennifer's husband of 15 years, had been unfaithful. Not once, but on many occasions. He ran away with another woman leaving Jennifer and two children in Texas. Frankie and John went to be with her as much as they could. They learned that James and Jennifer were deeply in debt. Frankie and John had to pay all of her legal expenses. They invited her and the children to come live with them, but she had grown up living in the parsonage and did not want any more of that life. Also, she did not want to leave Texas.

Then it was Frank's turn, the oldest child. Frank married Cheryl Presley, his high school sweetheart, just after college graduation. After law school, they moved to Florida to join a firm involved in real estate speculations.

That was the first of a series of bad business relationships for Frank. Things were settling down with Jennifer when Frank, Cheryl, and the three children came for a visit. Frank and John were in the pastor's study at the church when Frank broke the news that they were on the verge of losing everything.

His explanation this time was just like the other times: it was not his fault. If his partners had done their part, if the economy hadn't turned bad, if interest rates hadn't changed; if... It was never his responsibility, not entirely.

The money John and Frankie gave Frank wiped out their savings. It was only enough to stave off immediate bankruptcy, and it was given on the condition that Frank and Cheryl enter financial counseling to get their spending under control and their lifestyle in line with their income. They resented it.

"You've got to stop the bleeding," John said aloud, then startled awake.

~~~~~

Lisa, holding a book she had taken off one of the shelves, looked at him from across the room. "Dreaming again?" she asked.

John regained his awareness of where he actually was.

"Nightmares," John answered.

7

THE APPOINTMENT

It was August second. John and Frankie, along with Senator Joe Holloway and his wife Marilyn, were ushered into the Vice President's Senate office.

The Constitution makes the Vice President of the United States the President or presiding officer of the Senate. Thus, he has a Senate office, but it is rarely used. The Vice President is also a member of the Executive Branch, and his regular office is in the West Wing of the White House.

Since the founding of our government, the role of the Vice President has changed. Early Vice Presidents were active in the day to day running of the Senate, with the exception of Thomas Jefferson who stayed in Virginia during his four years as VP. Today, the majority party appoints a President Pro Tempore who does most of the presiding. The Majority Leader does the day to day running of the Senate's business. The Vice President shows up mainly for ceremonial events and only votes in the event of a tie, and that rarely happens.

The office of the Vice President of the United States is a serious position, being first in the line of succession to the President, but it can also be a very frustrating position. In modern times Vice Presidents are not chosen according to their ability to govern but according to their ability to bring in votes and money. This was precisely the case for Jim Simpson.

Bill Tate was going to win the party's nomination. Simpson had given him a run for his money, but now it was time to focus on winning in November. Tate offered Simpson the Vice Presidency. Simpson, a former governor of Georgia, brought the southern vote to the ticket. But even more critical, Simpson brought in H. J. Troxell.

Howard Jordan Troxell was an elusive Atlanta-based business giant. Born to immigrant parents from the Philippines, he grew up dirt poor. He became one of the wealthiest men in the world with a fortune estimated at nearly a trillion dollars. He was also one of the most private men in the world. Troxell was of average height and build and kept himself in top physical condition. People who met him would never guess he was nearly 80 years old. His black hair was combed straight back with a wet look that made him look like some sort of mafia king, which he was. He had the manicured look of wealth, always with a beautiful woman at his side in public. But he had never married, nor admitted to any children, though there were rumors.

His business dealings were vast. Troxco Industries had interests in weapons development, advanced technology, energy, and vast real-estate holdings on a worldwide scale. Quietly, he was involved in politics.

Troxell had backed Simpson in his two runs as governor of Georgia and had bankrolled his unsuccessful race for the party's presidential nomination. President Bill Tate put up with Vice President Jim Simpson—who he personally did not like—in order to tap into the resources of H.J. Troxell. This left Jim Simpson with a frustrating job.

Jim Simpson and Joe Holloway became friends when they both served as southern governors. They and their wives enjoyed being in Washington together.

In April, The Reverend Doctor Robert James Smith announced his plans to retire as Senate Chaplain after 12 years, to take effect at the start of the summer recess.

Congressional chaplains have historically been non-partisan. However, in the previous decade, the majority party in the House of Representatives had changed every two years for eight years running. The constant turnover and the influence of the bitter Denominational Wars resulted in the politicization of the office of House Chaplain. Thus, the House did away with the office of chaplain.

In the Senate, however, the office of chaplain continued. With Dr. Smith's retirement, there was a cry to follow the House and eliminate the office of chaplain in the Senate also. That was not going to be.

It would not have been the first time the offices of Chaplain had been eliminated from Congress. In the 1850s, after the positions became politicized over slavery, both the House and Senate removed them. For a brief period the chambers relied on local pastors to lead the opening prayer of each session, but it didn't last. The office of chaplain for both the House and the Senate was soon restored.

Troxell saw an opportunity in the coming vacancy. A red-hot controversy around the office of chaplain in the Senate could be a useful distraction. He instructed a number of his people in various states to find a candidate for chaplain who would suit his needs.

Bob Burns, who worked for Troxell, came up with the Reverend Doctor John A. Grant. Troxell signed off on it. Burns made a timely suggestion to Senator Joe Holloway, who nominated John for the office. Troxell made sure that Vice President Jim Simpson was on board.

John received a phone call.

Three months later he and Frankie, along with Joe and Marilyn Holloway were on their way into the Vice President's ceremonial office in the Capitol. It was appointment day.

A resolution appointing John was pushed through the Senate. Before the flash of cameras, Vice President Jim Simpson presented a framed copy of the resolution to John and Frankie. Congress went into summer recess the next day. On September the 9th they returned. John and Frankie had a month to get ready for the start of their new life.

Nothing in their previous experiences prepared them for the storm that was to come.

8

THE DENOMINATIONAL WARS

"Pastor John, I hate to appear stupid, but I have a question," Lisa said as John told her about the different photos and mementos in the study.

"There is no such thing as a stupid question, Lisa. You can ask me anything."

"Okay, you've used the words Denominational Wars several times. I really don't know what it means. Is it something like the Civil War, only between the Baptists and the Methodists?"

"No," John chuckled. "It's like, well, let's see. How do I describe this to you?"

"It's alright," Lisa said. "I don't have to know."

"I want you to know about it. Look in that filing cabinet beside you, in the second drawer, I think. See if you can find a folder labeled 'Denominational Wars.'"

Lisa turned around, slid open the second drawer and began thumbing through the files.

"Here it is," she said. She pulled out a thick folder, full of clippings and other pages.

"That's it," John said. "Put it on the desk."

He opened the folder and began shuffling through the pages.

"Here it is!" he exclaimed. He handed her a photocopy of a newspaper article.

Lisa took it and looked it over. "What is this?" she asked.

"It's a column by a *Chicago Tribune* columnist named Jerry Spraberry. The column is called 'Spray Berries,' which is a play on his name.

John paused. Lisa looked up from the page at him. "Is that supposed to be funny?" she asked.

John looked at her. "Uh... yes, it is. Never mind. He wrote about this suburban, Pentecostal megachurch—it's more like a cult. They had someone on staff that had abused some children. People who complained had been driven out of the church. They joined a nearby denominational church and started a prayer meeting for those still in the cult.

"Spraberry, who hates religion, thought it was absurd, that former members of one church were praying for members of another church to leave that church. He wrote this column about it."

Lisa continued looking at the old photocopy, shrugged her shoulders and said, "Okay."

"Look, read the part that is highlighted, and maybe you'll understand.

Lisa found it and began reading aloud. "It's not enough that some fundamentalist groups refuse to jettison old-fashioned beliefs that have been swept away by more progressive believers willing to bow to modernity; now some are actively organizing prayer groups to pray their friends out of one cult and into another. They call it 'spiritual warfare.' I'll call it what it is, 'denominational wars,' and will gladly sit on the sidelines and enjoy watching these people self-destruct."

Lisa looked up with a bewildered look on her face. "I don't get it," she said.

"It's alright," John said. "Don't worry about it." How could he explain the insanity of all that happened?

He told her how the column went viral on social media. Spraberry was invited to late-night TV and other entertainment-news outlets where he repeated the phrase, and a new Spray-Berry phrase was born: "The Denominational Wars."

"You see Lisa, giving something a name can somehow give it a life. The Pentecostal pastor responded with his own BlogSpot in which he viciously attacked the former members and the little Nazarene Church they now attended. Religious radio and television, along with Internet outlets, picked up on it and gave him a platform. He encouraged the members of that church, and of all Nazarene churches, to leave.

"'Don't just leave,' he wrote. 'Run out the door as fast as you can while there is still time to save yourselves and your families.'"

John continued, "That pastor of that little Nazarene Church didn't know what hit him. The next Sunday news reporters with cameras showed up outside his church door looking for a response and a story."

He told her how denominational leaders stepped in to handle the controversy. Since he was the current president of his denomination, he had to issue a response. Then sexual abuse advocates jumped in, along with LGBT activists who saw an opportunity, and anti-religion zealots who never missed a chance to spotlight anything negative associated with religion. Soon other denominational leaders were weighing in, and then the major media outlets picked up on the story.

Charges of sheep stealing, of discrimination, of homophobia, of covering up sexual abuse, of prejudice by mainline denominational churches against independent churches, of spiritual superiority by independent churches against mainline churches flew across social media. It filled the pages of newspapers, flooded the blogosphere, and dominated the airways. The talking heads bobbled incessantly.

"The fire ignited so fast and furiously, within a week *The New York Times* had a front-page article with the headline 'The Denominational Wars.' And it was on," John said.

Lisa was dumbfounded. She knew of none of this. "I guess this was during the time when I was using drugs. When you're doing drugs, you're very self-centered. All you can think about is how you're going to get your next fix. The house could burn down around you, and you'd barely notice."

"Later that year, when the Supreme Court legalized same-sex marriage in the United States, things heated up even more," John said. "Over the next several years a massive change in attitudes toward organized religion crystalized. For traditional denominational churches like First Church, it was the beginning of a very difficult period.

"That's the Denominational Wars in a nutshell."

"Ok," Lisa said. "I get it." But she really didn't.

PART TWO

The Wedding Trip

9

THE ENGAGEMENT

Josie was finishing her twice-weekly visit with Pastor John.

"Pastor," she said, shaking her head. "You're not improving. You could make progress if you would allow us to reschedule physical therapy."

John didn't say anything.

"Okay, be hard-headed. I can be just as hard-headed, you know," she said.

John still didn't speak.

His vital signs were actually okay, but he could improve his general health if he would just let her bring back the physical therapist.

After his stroke, John spent thirty days in a swing bed. Jennifer and her sister-in-law Cheryl took turns staying with him, and when he went home, Rachel came for a few weeks. Bob Burns had first hired Josie when Frankie had been diagnosed with pancreatic cancer. Bob called her back to help John with his post-stroke recovery.

He made good progress at first, enough so that Rachel felt she could return to Africa as long as competent sitters were there to help. With physical therapy coming three days a week, there was every reason to think John would regain much of what he had lost due to the stroke.

Then John suddenly told the PT people not to come back. He ran off his first sitter, then a second, and a third after only two days. Josie told Bob Burns she felt like the Pastor wanted to die. Coldly, Bob Burns said that would be okay with him.

Then Lisa came to sit with him. The first few days were rough—Pastor John put her through whatever it was he put the others through, but she seemed to have passed the test. John was better emotionally, but he was not improving physically.

"Why don't you let me schedule PT again?"

John still said nothing.

Josie looked at him. Finally, she got up and said, "Well, I'm not a social worker, I'm a healthcare professional. You do what you want. You always do anyway."

John reached out and took her hand. She stopped and turned back to him.

"Thank you," he said softly.

Josie melted. "You're welcome, Pastor. I only want you to get better."

They exchanged a look, and then Josie rushed out the door.

Last week Pastor John had agreed to a short walk in the garden. The day was beautiful. Lisa thought maybe he would like to do that again.

"How about we go down and enjoy the garden again?" she asked.

"You need to clean up after lunch," he said. They had just finished eating when Josie came in.

"It's not going anywhere. I can do that later," she said.

She hoped he would agree. The house had beautiful formal gardens in the back. A professional landscape service kept the gardens in shape all year round. The concrete walkway made it easy for John to move among the different sections. There was a fountain, a goldfish pond, several benches to rest on and an arbor to escape the hot sun.

The lawn sections were perfectly manicured. Topiaries gave vertical accents. Roses, tulips, asters, camellias and dozens of other flowers were perfectly spaced between beautifully maintained boxwood hedges that lined the wandering trail. A beautiful magnolia tree was like a centerpiece, with several huge live oaks along the sides, and bordering the back boundary were crepe myrtles of alternating colors.

Sometimes when Pastor John was resting, Lisa would sit in the swing beneath one of the live oaks or read in the arbor. There was even an outdoor fireplace, which she hoped, come fall she would get to enjoy.

While she was waiting for John to respond, the house computer chimed in.

"There is a phone call from Cheryl Grant's cell phone. Would you like to take it?"

Pastor John said nothing.

Lisa thought about it a minute. She had not talked to this part of his family. It was time she did.

"Yes, I'll take it," Lisa said.

She heard the phone come alive and she said out loud, "Hello, Pastor John Grant's residence."

There was a pause.

"Okay, who is this?" the woman's voice asked impatiently.

"I'm Lisa Smithy. I'm Pastor John's day sitter," Lisa said.

"Well, I need to talk to John—not the hired help. Can you give him a handset?" She was very abrupt.

Lisa felt her face redden as tears immediately stung her eyes.

John spoke up. "It's okay Cheryl. Lisa is like family to me. We can talk like this."

You could tell his daughter-in-law did not approve, but she cleared her throat and went on.

"Okay John, whatever you say. I've got some good news. Maybe this will cheer you up!" she said.

John thought to himself, "I doubt it." But he said, "Great. What's up?"

"Olivia is getting married," she said excitedly. "Logan popped the question over the weekend while they were in Aruba."

John again thought to himself one thing and said another. He thought, "It's about time. They've been living together for several years." He said, "That's wonderful news. I'm so excited for Olive Oil. Tell her I think that's great news." Olive Oil had been his nickname for her since she was a baby. Cheryl didn't like it. Olivia loved it.

"That's not her name, John," Cheryl said with an annoyed sound in her voice.

"Have they set a date yet?" John asked.

"I know this is kind of quick," Cheryl said, "but they want to get married on August 12th."

Lisa thought to herself, "Three and a half months. Is that quick enough?"

John said, "That is rather quick."

Cheryl jumped right on it. "She's not pregnant John. I know that's what you're thinking. And you might as well know she's not getting married in a church. She wants to have her wedding at the Botanical Gardens in Port St. Lucie."

"That's perfectly fine with me," John said. He was not surprised, but he was disappointed that Frank and Cheryl had not raised their three children in the church. Now it was time for the next shoe to drop.

"Now, John," Cheryl began.

Here it comes, John thought.

"Given your physical condition, we are not asking you to do the wedding. As a matter of fact, Olivia will understand if you are not able to come at all," she said.

Lisa looked at John. That had to be disappointing, but frankly, she wondered if he was physically able to go.

John's face did not register any response. He said, "That's okay, but I will be there. You tell Olive Oil that I would not miss her wedding for anything."

Olivia broke in. "Granddaddy, I am sooo glad to hear you say that. I want you to be here. I miss you so much."

At the sound of her voice, John broke into a big grin.

"I wouldn't miss it for the world, Olive Oil," he said. "You know, you could have your wedding here. We have big formal gardens. It is a perfect spot for a wedding," he said.

Cheryl spoke up. "That decision has already been made. We've put down a deposit at the Botanical Gardens and for condos at a nearby golf resort," she said.

"This sounds like it will be expensive," John said. Frank and Cheryl had always lived way beyond their means.

Cheryl said, "Don't worry about that. Bob Burns said he would help take care of things."

Lisa saw John's expression change. She saw a flash of anger.

"Of course," was all John said.

Lisa wondered, "What is the hold Bob Burns has on Pastor John and his family?"

Pastor John and his wife were given this incredible house to live in after they returned from Washington. She believed all the bills were paid, including utilities, professional landscaping, and a cleaning service. Her check every two weeks was very generous, and it was from Burns and Associates, not from John Grant. The memo line said House Account.

Mr. Burns had repeatedly told her to get whatever John needed and use the debit card he had given her, and not to worry about any expenses. Pastor John had never said anything about his financial position and she certainly never asked. When she first started, she thought, given the house, that he was well off, but Lisa had gotten the impression that he was not at all wealthy. It was strange that he lived off the generosity of someone who didn't seem to be a generous person.

At first, she thought it was just kindness on Bob Burns' part. She soon came to realize that he was not a kind man. She didn't understand the relationship between Pastor John and Bob Burns, and she couldn't stand to see Pastor John look upset. She would have to ask.

John asked, "Are you inviting Jennifer, Rachel, and Ben?"

"Of course," Cheryl answered annoyed. "Ben said he wouldn't be coming. No surprise there. Jennifer and the kids will be there, and this will make you happy—Rachel is coming."

"I'm going to be happy to see all of you," John responded. "Tell me, is Bob paying everyone's expenses for coming?" he asked.

There was silence.

"Never mind," John said. "I'm excited for Olivia. And I will be there."

"Whatever," Cheryl said, and she hung up.

Lisa stood next to John with her mouth open. "Jiminy Cricket! That was rude," she said.

"That's Cheryl," John said.

Lisa stood with her left hand on her hip. "Pastor, what is it with Bob Burns? What is going on here?" she asked.

John spoke as he signaled to her to get him paper and pen.

"Bob advises me concerning all my affairs. He has been a great help and friend for many years," he said in a normal tone.

Lisa handed him a pad and a pen. He wrote. "Not in the house!!!"

Lisa stared at the note as a look of astonishment crossed her face. Was the house listening? Bob Burns was listening? She suddenly had a hundred questions. She suddenly felt like someone was watching. How had Frankie and John lived there? She looked at John.

John held his finger to his lips. Then he said. "Call Josie. Tell her to schedule physical therapy. I've got three months to get ready to go to Florida for a wedding."

10

THE CASH

There had been quite a discussion about how to get John to Port St. Lucie, Florida. Frank and Cheryl teamed up with Bob Burns to insist John fly down. There were no direct flights from the capital city. As they say about flying in the south, it doesn't matter if you're going to heaven or hell; you've got to go through Atlanta.

John didn't want to fly.

Frank offered to fly his 24-year-old son Jacob up, and Jacob could drive him down, drive him back and then fly back home. Jacob didn't really want to do all of that. Of his five grandchildren, Jacob was the one who never seemed to care about visiting with John and Frankie. As John described Jacob and how he was meandering through life, Lisa said, "He's a drug user." John looked at her, puzzled.

John insisted Lisa drive them. It was about a ten-hour drive. They could break it up over two days and only have to drive about five hours a day going down. Rachel would come back with them and could share the driving with Lisa on the return trip.

Bob Burns finally agreed but said he wanted to put the mini-van in the shop before the trip to make sure it was travel worthy.

That van was only a couple of years old. John figured Bob Burns would be placing some kind of listening device in the van, so he started making other plans.

About a month before the trip John called his former associate, Mike Summers.

"Mike? John."

"John, how are you today?" Mike asked.

"I'm feeling better than I have in a while, Mike. As a matter of fact, I feel so good I was wondering if you and Jane would take me to church with you Sunday?" John asked. They were scheduled to sit with him this coming Sunday anyway. They always missed church to help him.

Mike said, "Hey, that's great. We will come by, say about 9:30, and I'll help you get ready. Is that okay?"

"Just come at about 10:00 and I'll be ready," John answered.

"He sounds like his old self," Mike thought to himself.

After John resigned and went to Washington, Mike helped transition First Church to a new pastor. As everything had changed at First Church, Mike was the holdover from the way the church had once been. That was a tough position.

When John had to abruptly resign the Senate chaplaincy, and he and Frankie returned from D.C. to live in the house, Mike and Jane had done everything they could to help them. They were very close, more than just colleagues.

When Frankie got sick Mike took his retirement from First Church and he and Jane helped in every way they could. Mike officiated Frankie's funeral.

After retiring from First Church it was impossible for him and Jane to continue to worship there, so after a few weeks, they joined Calvary Church, an old-line denominational church near their home on the east side of town. Though Frankie and John kept their membership at First Church, they too could not return there for worship.

This was hard for some people to understand, but Frankie and John could not enter that beautiful Gothic sanctuary without being flooded with memories and overwhelmed with the subtle and not too subtle complaints about the new pastor. For that pastor's sake and for the church's sake, they needed to stay out of the way.

Fortunately, John had plenty of invitations to preach. When John was not preaching somewhere, he and Frankie would visit their children, or they would join Jane and Mike at Calvary. After Frankie died, John would occasionally worship with them. Since the stroke, he had not been able to attend at all.

True to his word John was ready when Mike and Jane arrived Sunday morning. They were amazed at how much progress he had made.

After worship, they went to the hospital cafeteria for lunch. Many current and former First Church members stopped by to talk. As they finished the meal, John leaned over to Mike and asked, "Is there somewhere we can go and talk privately?"

Mike looked over at Jane. "You are welcome to come over to our house for the afternoon," he said.

"I don't want to be an imposition," he said looking at Jane.

"John Grant," she said scolding. "You're family. We are alone this weekend, but even if we weren't, we would love for you to come over."

Mike and Jane's son and family lived near New Orleans. Sometimes they or their grandchildren visit on weekends. "Gratefully, not this weekend," John thought to himself.

While at the Summers' house John pulled a couple pages of hand-written notes from his coat pocket and gave them to Mike. Mike read them all, then handed the pages to Jane. She read them. They looked at each other and nodded.

"You've got it, Buddy," Mike said. "You know, whatever we can do to help, we are there for you."

They shook hands and then went over the details.

On a shopping trip about two weeks from the trip, John asked Lisa to go to a different bank than usual. At the bank, John gave Lisa a personal debit card and his picture ID. He told her to go to the drive-through window and ask to withdraw $10,000 cash.

Lisa looked at him. "Are you sure about this, Pastor John?" she asked.

"Yes," he said.

Lisa passed the card and ID over to the teller and made the request. A moment later the branch vice president was at the window. "For such a large withdrawal we need you to come inside," he said.

"No, we don't, Bill," John responded. "You can handle this for me."

Bill leaned down so he could see who was in the passenger's seat. He recognized John. "Are you sure, Pastor," Bill said. "I don't know this woman."

"It's fine, Bill. This is Lisa Smithy; she helps me out at home. Guess what, Bill. Olivia is getting married. We are going to Florida for her wedding next week. I want to give them a really nice gift."

Bill looked at John, then at Lisa. "Okay, but I need to see her ID, too."

"Okay, Bill. Whatever you say." Then he said to Lisa, "Get your driver's license and give it to him," John said.

Lisa hesitated. She turned to John and spoke quietly. "There may be a problem here," she said.

"What's the problem?" John asked.

"My driver's license is from Oregon."

"Is it current?" John asked.

"For two more years," Lisa responded.

Bill spoke over the intercom. "Is there a problem?" he asked.

John waved his hand at Lisa to answer him.

"No problem," she said. She got out her driver's license and placed it in the drawer.

Bill looked at her license, then looked at Lisa. He told the teller to make a photocopy of it. He smiled at John and said, "You be careful with that kind of money." Then he added, "Have a good trip, Pastor."

A cash withdrawal check was given to her for John to sign.

The teller asked, "How do you want it?"

Lisa turned to John, "How do we want it?"

"Seven thousand in one hundred dollar bills, one thousand in fifties, the rest in twenties and tens," John said.

Lisa passed on the information. As they waited, she looked at John. "What is this?" she asked.

"I want to give my grandkids some money, and we might need some spending money," he said with a wink.

"But I have the debit card Mr. Burns gave me. He said I can use it for anything we need," she responded.

"This account belongs to me. It is private. Bob Burns doesn't need to know about it," he said. "Okay?"

Lisa shrugged her shoulders. "Okay."

A moment later the teller gave her two manila envelopes stuffed with $5,000 each. Lisa tried to hand it to John, but he told her to keep it for him.

Her hand shook as she stuffed the envelopes in her purse. She had never held that kind of money before, not even when she was selling drugs.

She thought about it every day, the calm that would immediately wash over her when she took the pills. Of course, she knew the calm would soon be replaced by a drug-induced paranoia. She didn't want to use again, but like most addicts, she thought about it. Having that kind of cash frightened her.

It was as if John could read her thoughts. "I trust you, Lisa. God will give you the strength you need," he said.

Lisa nodded her head and put her purse back on the floor. She looked up at John. Two months of physical therapy was showing on his face. His color was better, his eyes clearer. Before, he shuffled around the house pushing his walker. Now he was walking around the house using only a cane.

Lisa and Josie, the healthcare professional, had talked one day while John was with the physical therapist. His stroke had been major, but he got to the ER in less than an hour after he fell. The house system was programmed to sense if someone falls. When John did not respond, the computer called 911. A tissue plasminogen activator was administered almost immediately. John should have recovered quickly and almost completely.

However, there were two complications. First, they discovered John had a heart valve issue. His heartbeat had been irregular for a while. He had not told anyone. If it had been discovered before the stroke, they could have repaired the valve or replaced it. Because of the stroke, he was not considered a good candidate for this kind of surgery.

The second complication was that John did not want to get better. The doctors prescribed a mood lifter to deal with his depression, but John stopped taking it, just as he refused the physical therapy.

The news about Olivia's wedding had energized him. Now he wanted to get better. Josie was pleased, but she warned Lisa. "John is a ticking bomb. That valve is going to calcify at some point, and he will be totally disabled. He won't survive long after that," she said. "The PT has probably bought him some more time, but you have to be careful. Don't let him push himself too hard. Give him plenty of time to rest."

Lisa promised she would. Lisa also sensed there was more to his newfound energy than just his granddaughter's wedding.

About ten days before the trip John called Bob Burns.

"Bob? This is John. I need to ask you something," he said.

Bob responded. "Okay. What's up? What do you need?"

"You know I've been going through my files and papers in the study," he said. "I've put together some old sermons into what I think will make a couple of books. Mike Summers has been helping me compile and edit the material. Is there any reason why he can't come over here while I'm gone and work some in the study?"

"None that I can think of," Bob said. "He has a passkey. Just be sure to let the front gate know he is coming."

"I don't want him to startle anyone or be surprised by anyone. Is there any scheduled maintenance going on that week?" John asked.

"Yes," Bob replied. "I've got the tech people coming on the Monday after the wedding to do some upgrades to the systems while you are gone," Bob said.

"Is it going to change how the system works? Are they going to mess up Freda?" John asked as if he cared.

"No, you won't notice anything. It's just time for some upgrades and to replace some old sensors. It's not anything important," Bob answered.

"Okay," John said. "I'll let Mike know."

That afternoon before she left, John gave Lisa a note. It said to call Mike Summers from her home phone and simply tell him, "Tuesday."

Bob Burns looked at his iPhone. He had been sent a text message that John had withdrawn $10,000 from his private bank account. Probably the money is a gift for the newlyweds. But could it be something else?

Bob was glad he planned to install a bug in the van for this trip. If something's up, they would surely talk about it on the way to the wedding. He had his bases covered.

11

THE RENTAL

Wednesday, the morning of their departure had arrived. Lisa put their bags in the back of the mini-van. Bob had somebody get the van Monday morning, and it had been returned ready to go on Tuesday afternoon. The trip would take two days down. The wedding was Saturday evening. They would stay Sunday and Monday to visit with family, then start the two-day trip home with Rachel. They would be back on Wednesday of the next week.

Lisa put his wheelchair and walker in, just in case they were needed. John had asked her a couple of days ago what kind of music she liked.

"Country," she replied with a swing of her hips.

"Then bring several of your favorite CDs or downloads, or whatever you call them today. We will plug them into the van's sound system and enjoy music all the way to Florida," he said.

So she did. She brought an iPod loaded with country music.

John didn't care for country music, but it didn't matter. The music was part of the plan.

John climbed into the passenger's seat and buckled his seatbelt. Lisa got behind the wheel, and they backed out. She ordered the garage door shut and the house secured, and off they went. John said, "Give us some music and make it loud!"

Lisa selected a playlist of some of her favorite songs. The first cut was a song by Jason Isbell and the Drive-by Truckers from back in 2012, "Decoration Day."

They passed through the front gate as the music started blaring on the van's music system. John handed her a piece of paper and held his finger to his mouth to not say anything. It was directions.

She started to enter the address into the GPS system, but John waved his hand and shook his head "no." So Lisa held the directions in her hand as she drove the van.

They got on the by-pass loop and took an exit two miles to the south. They went about five miles east on that road, then turned into a middle-class neighborhood filled with green lawns and ranch style homes.

They pulled up into the driveway of Mike and Jane Summers.

John indicated to her to keep the van running, to leave the remote key on the seat and to let the music play as she got out. He got out also, as quietly as he could.

Mike came out of the house. There was a rented SUV in the driveway. Mike gave Lisa the key to the rental and then began quietly transferring the luggage from the mini-van as the music blared.

John said to Lisa, "Give him the envelope with the one thousand dollars in it."

Mike said, "John, that's not necessary."

"I told you I would take care of everything. Oh, by the way, it's all country music, and you'll have to speak quietly the whole time, but have a nice trip to Port St. Lucie," John said.

Lisa looked inquisitively at them. "If they are going to Port St. Lucie, then where are we going?" she asked.

"We are going to Port St. Lucie, too, only we are going in the rental." John pointed to it. He added, "You'll have to leave your country music with them. If Bob Burns checks the GPS on the min-van, it went to Port St. Lucie, Florida. If anyone is listening, they'll hear country music for two days. And if anyone asks, Mike and Jane were invited to the wedding, which they were, and they went."

Lisa continued to be confused. "We are not going in the van?" she asked.

John answered as he climbed in the passenger side of the rental. "It's bugged. Why do you think Bob Burns took it for almost two days? I want us to be able to talk without anyone else listening."

Lisa looked at the mini-van. "Jiminy Cricket! It's bugged?"

About that time a young man with long hair and a scraggly beard came out of Mike and Jane's house carrying some kind of device.

"This is Will Blakely, the guy I told you about," Mike said. "That wand he is carrying detects electronic transmissions."

The young man waved it around and over the top of the mini-van. He turned back to them grinning like a Cheshire cat. The red light on top of the wand was flashing like a beacon. "It's hot," he said.

Lisa climbed in and started the rental. As they backed out, Jane emerged from the house rolling a suitcase and waving. Mike loaded it into the still running, country music blaring mini-van.

John spoke. "We're going to the same hotel for tonight, but we won't be traveling together."

Lisa said, "I don't understand all of this."

John leaned his seat back and settled in. "I've got to rest a bit. We have plenty of time to talk. I've got a story to tell you that you won't believe. You can't ever tell it to anyone, and when I am finished, I need to ask you to do something for me. It's not illegal, but there may be people who, if they knew about it, would try and stop you. You'll have to decide if you are willing to help me or not."

John shut his eyes to rest. Lisa's eyes were wide open. "What in the world was this all about?" she wondered.

~~~~~

John dreamed about Frankie. She was in bed at the house. John was in a chair at her side, holding her hand. Frank, Jennifer, and Rachel were all there. Josie was there. Mike and Jane were in the next room. Cheryl and all five grandchildren were downstairs.

The kitchen door chimed. Ben walked into the bedroom. Robert, his partner, was behind him.

Rachel turned and embraced Ben. As she held him, he looked at his mother in the bed, dying. His eyes filled with tears and he began sobbing.

Ben pushed past Rachel, Jennifer, and Frank. He moved past John who stood to embrace him. Ben fell to his knees at his mother's side and wailed out loud.

Jennifer left the room. Frank turned to the corner. Rachel stood at the other side of the bed. Robert came around to the side to where John stood.

John and Robert embraced.

"Thank you for bringing him," John said and wept.

Robert held him.

Ben hardly moved from her side for two days.

There was one moment when she opened her eyes and was aware of her surroundings. "Ben, my baby," she said through dried, cracked lips.

Those were her last words.

~~~~~

The van hit a bump. John startled awake. He remembered where he was.

Lisa asked, "Are you okay? You were making noises."

John smacked his lips and reached for the water in the cup holder between the seats.

"Yes," he said after a couple of swallows. "Just remembering why I have to do this."

"What is it we are doing?" Lisa asked.

John said nothing, just stared straight ahead.

"By the way, Mike and Jane passed us about half an hour ago. They waved. Looked like they were enjoying my music," she said.

John smiled. Mike hates country music, too. What a friend.

"Can we make a stop soon?" John asked.

"I thought you would never ask," she replied.

Lisa headed up the next exit to an Exxon station. She let John out near the store, then she pulled the SUV over to get gas.

She bounced up and down as the gas finished pumping. She met John as he came out of the store. "Do you want anything?" she asked as they passed.

"M&Ms," John replied.

Lisa finished her business; got some M&Ms for John and a cup of coffee for herself, paid for them and was back in the van.

"We've got about three more hours," she said. She wanted to push him to fess up, but she had learned this about John; he will tell you what he wants you to know when he wants you to know it.

John suggested they get some lunch just down the road at a buffet. They enjoyed the meal, and then they got back on the road.

After a few miles, John finally spoke.

12

THE TRAP

"When we got to D.C., Frankie and I had high expectations of the good we could do. Our prayer was that from the position of Chaplain of the Senate we could help mend the rifts caused by the Denominational Wars.

"We were very naive. The housing costs in D.C. were astronomical. After my appointment ceremony, the Vice President pulled me aside and told me he knew of a man who owned a really nice townhouse in Georgetown and that he might let us live there. I thought he meant let us rent it. One of the Vice President's aides took us over there that afternoon. It was fabulous; three stories plus a basement, four bedrooms, five baths, completely furnished, a gated, secure parking area in the back, and twenty-four-hour security."

John continued, "The aide said we could put our own furniture in storage and just move in it as it was. Frankie asked what if she wanted some of our own things. The aide said to pick out the rooms where we wanted our own furniture, and he would have those rooms emptied, and our furniture moved in."

"I finally asked how much the monthly rent would be. The aide said zero. He said the man who owns it rarely uses it himself. It's for leasing or for VIPs he occasionally sends to Washington. He has other properties. He was happy to allow us to utilize it for as long as we were in Washington. Or, we could just try it for a few weeks or months, and if we didn't like it, we could find another place.

"'There is one more thing,' the aide said, 'It includes a cleaning service.'"

"Frankie and I looked at each other. This was too good to be true. I asked the aide who the owner was. He said he was not at liberty to say, only that it was a faithful patriot."

"We told him we would think about it and returned to our hotel. That evening the Vice President called.

"He said, 'Dr. Grant, did you like the townhouse?'"

"I told him we did, but I didn't think we could accept that kind of generosity."

"He said, 'Of course you can. Everyone in Washington does. It's the only way normal people can afford to live here. Just ask Joe if you have any questions,' and he hung up."

"So I called my best friend, Senator Joe Holloway. He told me I was crazy not to accept the offer. I asked him who the owner was and he said it didn't matter. Washington was full of generous people who loved the Lord and loved the country.

"'Don't look a gift horse in the mouth,' Joe said. 'Just accept it.'"

"We did. The next Sunday I resigned at First Church, and we had most of our things put in storage. The Senate paid to move our bedroom furniture, one guest room of furniture, and Frankie's sewing room furniture to D.C."

"We didn't realize it, but at that point, we were trapped," John said.

"I don't understand," Lisa said. "How were you trapped?"

"We were living off the generosity of someone we didn't know," John explained. "As things unfolded, we were soon dependent on that generosity. That's not a good place to be."

"But you said that you guys had always lived in a parsonage. That's a home the church provides. Isn't that the same thing?" Lisa asked.

"Not at all," John answered. "When a pastor lives in a parsonage, he knows exactly who is providing that house and what the expectations are. Often there is a written agreement about how the house is to be maintained and what happens if the pastor were to resign and so forth."

"The house I am in now," John continued, "it is provided for us at no cost. Everything happened so fast that I never asked the questions I should have asked. Bob Burns was there assuring me it was all okay, and just to trust him. The next thing we knew Frankie was sick and, well, I'm still in the house."

Lisa said, "So the owner of the house is the same person who owned the townhouse."

John looked over at her. "Yes," he said.

"And it is not Bob Burns?"

"No, it is not Bob Burns," John said.

"Jiminy Cricket," Lisa said. "Then who is it?"

John looked at the road ahead. He had never told anyone this. Never. But Lisa was the one he could trust. He was sure of it.

"H. J. Troxell," John said after a few moments.

Lisa didn't say anything. Then she made a funny face. "Who's that?" she asked.

John couldn't believe it. "Only one of the richest, most powerful men in the world," John answered.

Lisa drove on for a few moments. She didn't know what the Denominational Wars were. She doesn't know who H. J. Troxell is. Why was she so uninformed of things in life? It made her feel inadequate. "Okay, so a rich man was nice to you. You're a pastor. Isn't it your job to encourage people to give? What's the big deal?" she asked.

"Well, first of all, the whole arrangement was a setup. Frankie and I and our children were all deeply hurt by what happened over those seven months. Troxell was responsible for it all. Second, my best friend, Joe Holloway, took the blame for something that happened in Washington D.C. which wasn't his fault. He died under that shadow. Troxell was responsible for all of that, too. And third, I am not supposed to know any of this."

"But you do know about it," Lisa said.

"Yes, I do," John answered.

"Okay, I'll bite. How do you know about all of this?" she asked.

"I can't say," John answered.

"Jiminy Cricket!" Lisa said with frustration. "What's with all the secrets? You know addiction loves secrets. It hides behind secrets."

"Well," John said, "Washington is addicted to power."

"And you are an enabler," she blurted out. "One of the keys to getting better is to get rid of all the family secrets. Let the light of truth in; air out the family laundry and all of that. Maybe you need to tell it all."

"It's not that simple," John said.

"Maybe it is and you are just making it hard. When it gets down to it, telling the truth is a simple act," Lisa said.

"No," John said. "It's not simple, because it involves people and people are not simple. People are complicated."

"People make things complicated. I'll grant you that Dr. Grant, but the truth is simple. You just tell it," Lisa said.

John thought for a moment. "I want the truth out, Lisa, but I am under a sacred obligation," John said.

"Jiminy Cricket!" Lisa rolled her eyes. "What is that some sort of masonic oath or something?" she asked. "I really don't understand what is so complicated about telling the truth."

John sighed in frustration.

"I'm not trying to be difficult Pastor John," Lisa said apologetically. "All this secret agent stuff is frightening me. Someone is listening to us at the house. We're supposed to be in the van Mike and Jane are in. They are listening to my music because the van is bugged and someone is listening there, too. And we are secretly riding in a rental. This is creepy!"

"I guess it is. I've been living with it a long time, and it's all new to you," he answered. "Let me try and explain it this way. When someone tells his lawyer something, that lawyer is sworn by his oath to the bar to keep that information confidential. Well, the same thing is true when someone tells a minister something within the confines of a pastor/parishioner relationship. A minister is obligated by his calling to God to keep that information confidential. I can't tell how I know what I know, but with your help, I think we can make certain information public without breaking that confidentiality," he said.

Lisa drove down the road, her mind trying to process all she had learned. She loved this job. She loved Pastor John, but she had no idea she was getting into something like this.

John closed his eyes and prayed. "Lord, she is the one. I'm sure she is. Help us both to find a way to do this."

They continued down I-75 toward central Florida. John was tired, and Lisa told him to rest.

Soon Lisa took the exit for the Holiday Inn Express where she had made reservations. She checked them into separate rooms. Then they went across the street to an *Outback Steak House* for dinner. Mike and Jane were waiting for them there. They enjoyed a good meal and the pleasure of friendly company.

Mike and Jane Summers were both in their 60s. She was a retired public-school teacher with soft grey hair that she wore shoulder length. Mike was nearly bald and as round as he was tall. As a hobby, he played the banjo with a Bluegrass band. They both had pleasing and quiet personalities. It was obvious how loyal Mike was to John.

John and Mike first met at a denominational event. They hit it off and soon after John asked Mike to join his staff at First Church as the Associate Pastor. This was more of an administrative position, for which Mike was well prepared, having earned an MBA as well as a seminary degree.

When Jane and Mike arrived at the capital city, she was expecting their first child. Two months later she had a miscarriage. Frankie and John walked with them through the entire ordeal, which sealed their friendship. A few years later they had a son. They remained close friends. Throughout Frankie's illness and death, Mike and Jane often held John up, spiritually and literally. Mike was John's best friend.

Mike helped John get settled into his room and into bed. Lisa was ready to get into her room and turn out the light. She was exhausted, but her mind was whirling. She didn't know if she could do what Pastor John was asking. She prayed for him and for whatever the future held. She prayed that she would find the assurance that she needed to help him.

By morning she had made up her mind. This was her calling now.

13

THE STORY

The next day after breakfast they continued their journey toward The Botanical Gardens of Port St. Lucie.

Lisa decided to start their conversation by asking a question. "Why was your time as Chaplain of the Senate so short?"

John's mind shot back to those heady days.

He explained that Congress returned from recess on September 9th. He and Frankie had moved into the townhouse a week prior. The opening session at the return from recess was his first opportunity to lead a prayer.

The chamber was full. Vice President Simpson presided. The President Pro-tempore was at his table, the majority leader beside him, and the minority leadership was at their table. Joe, John's best friend, stood with him near the podium.

Frankie sat in the gallery, along with Frank, Cheryl, and two of their children, Jennifer, and her two children, but not Ben. As usual, he stayed away. Rachel was saving her vacation for a more extended visit at Christmas, but she was watching on *C-Span* through the Internet.

The Vice President hammered his gavel, calling the Senate into session. He called on Joe Holloway to lead the chamber in the Pledge of Allegiance. Afterward the Vice President called the Reverend Dr. John Alexander Grant, the Senate's new Chaplain, to lead the opening prayer.

John cleared his throat. "You can't imagine what it felt like to stand at the podium before the United States Senate to lead in prayer," he said. "Matters of tremendous national and international urgency would be discussed and decided in that room. Former Presidents and the current President had been in that room. A future President was in that room."

"Frankie and I got right to work. I touched base with the existing Christian and non-Christian fellowship groups in the Senate. We organized new prayer and Bible study fellowships for Senate employees and staffers. We began having Senators and their spouses over for dinner or lunch. Overall we were warmly received."

"But I had a bigger agenda. I wanted to have a summit meeting of the leaders of the major denominations and associations of churches from across America. The Vice President and the Majority Leader gave me every encouragement."

"However, things turned out to be more difficult than I imagined. Immediately there was resistance. Everything was a debate. Who got to sit where at the table? Who was going to pay the expenses for all of these people to come? Who could they bring with them?"

"I've dealt with pastoral egos before. I served two years as president of my own denomination and chaired almost every committee. I was well aware of the raw ambition that some persons in the ministry carry, but I had never addressed anything like this."

"Pastor John, was it really that bad?" Lisa asked.

"Oh, it gets worse," John answered. "We had hoped to have that summit after the first of the year. It all fell apart before the end of September. I realized I was going to have to spend the better part of a year doing a lot of individual arm-twisting and ego smoothing in a series of smaller meetings in order to pull off the larger meeting."

"So, in mid-October, Frankie and I invited the executive of our denomination along with the heads of two other large groups for a few days as our guests in Washington. That was the first hint we had of the storm that was to come," he said. "What happened?" Lisa asked.

"We went to dinner that first night at a wonderful restaurant at Washington's historic Central Station. One of the men had been cordial but distant since he arrived. After we enjoyed our meal, I wanted to have a short, substantive conversation about my goals. That man dropped a bomb."

Lisa exclaimed, "A bomb!"

"Not a literal bomb," John said, "but it might as well have been."

"He took a sip of his wine and then he turned to Frankie and said, 'I understand you have a gay son?'"

"Frankie was taken back a bit. We did not discuss our children with people we did not know well. It was not that we were trying to hide anything; it just was easier not to go into all of the intricacies of their lives."

"Frankie told him that was true. That our youngest son Ben is gay, and he lives in California."

"The man then stated, 'Is it also true that when he came out you disowned him?' This was not said so much as a question as it was an accusation."

"Frankie told him no, that was not true."

"I interrupted. I told him that our son Ben had nothing to do with what we were trying to accomplish."

"He responded, 'But, it is true that your son is gay, he lives in California and that you and the rest of your family will not have anything to do with him.'"

"I told him this was not the issue we were there to discuss."

"He said, 'That is issue enough for us not to have any part of this.'"

"And with that, he stood and thanked us for the meal, but added that he and his wife would not be staying, and they left."

"Later that evening he would not accept my calls. Our other guests left the next day. Frankie and I were dumbfounded."

"Pastor John, I have to ask you," Lisa said. "Is it true? Is your son gay?"

"Yes," John answered. "He quit his job and moved out to California over ten years ago."

"Did you disown him?" Lisa asked. "Please tell me it's not true because if it is, well, I will have a hard time with that. It's not fair to treat a guy that way."

"Lisa," John answered, "do you think for one minute either Frankie or I would have treated any of our children that way?"

"Well, you are not particularly close to any of them, from what I can see," she said bluntly.

John sat in stony silence. The truth stung. He and Frankie had been successful in most everything they had ever done, except raising children. Frank was self-centered, materialistic and greedy. He and his family had no part in church-life. Jennifer was aloof and in permanent victim status. Since her divorce she too rarely attended church. Ben was gay and had disowned them, but strangely enough, regularly attended a gay-friendly church in the San Francisco area. Rachel at least embraced their passion for faith and service, but it was like she moved as far away from them as she could. His family did not present a pretty picture.

There was a long moment of awkward silence.

"I've got to take a break," Lisa announced. She headed up the next exit ramp. The truth was John needed a break, too.

Lisa got gas and they each visited the restroom and got a snack. Then they got back on the road.

"Lisa ..."

"Pastor..."

They spoke at the same time. It broke the ice. John told her, "You go first."

"Pastor, I don't mean to make any kind of accusations. I really don't know anything about your children or that much about you and Frankie. Please forgive me if I offended you," she said.

John said, "There's nothing to forgive. I'm asking a lot of you. You have a right to know about these things."

"I want you to understand this," he continued. "Frankie and I loved our children, without condition, but life in a parsonage can be hard. Too often the needs and desires of other families took priority over my own family. Frankie covered up for a lot of my failings, but in the end all our children were affected."

"People's expectations of a pastor and his family can be unrealistic. The pressure can be tremendous. Frankie and I came to accept the fish bowl life as part of the package deal, the cost of being called to ministry. We thought we handled it pretty well and that we shielded our children from it. As it turns out, we did not do a very good job. Each of our children walked away from life in the parsonage wounded in one way or another."

"You'll get to meet them all, except Ben, at the wedding," John said. "I need to let you form your own impressions about each of them."

Lisa said, "You know my mother talked of you and your family as if you were perfect. I mean, she thought you could walk on water."

"I never did master that one," John said.

Lisa giggled.

"Since he won't be at the wedding, I'll tell you about Ben. He has a magnetic personality. People are drawn to him. Ben lights up a room. When he was young, everyone said he would be the preacher in the family. As a child he told me he wanted to be a pastor, just like me. He was an excellent student. Like his mother, he loved literature."

"He seemed to be a normal adolescent. He was active in things at school and at church. He told us he was gay right after he graduated from the state university. I didn't see it coming. Frankie did, and she had been trying to get me to notice that something was happening to Ben. I was too busy as usual."

"That was a rough time. Ben decided to leave. We begged him not to."

John paused as he remembered those difficult days.

"Ben's partner, Robert Schroeder, is a really nice man," John said. "I wish you could meet both of them. Ben came back just before his mother died. Afterward, I went out there, several times, before suffering this stroke. With Robert's help I have made progress in my relationship with Ben."

"Please believe me, Lisa; we did not disown Ben," John said emphatically. "But the relationship has been strained for a long time."

"And why is that, Pastor John?" Lisa asked.

"It's because I will not accept that his homosexuality is a normal expression of human sexuality," he said.

"I don't know how to respond to that," Lisa said, puzzled.

"I realize that," John said with a sigh. "Amazingly, just a decade or so ago nobody would have been astonished by that point of view and most people would have been surprised by the opposite."

"Not in my generation," Lisa responded.

"That is true. Your generation is the hinge around which society's view of sexuality has turned. Before your generation came of age, it was unthinkable to call lesbian, gay, bi-sexual or transsexual as normal, and when asked, the majority would have said that marriage is between a man and a woman. All of that changed quickly."

"And people like you got caught on the wrong side of the fence," Lisa said, thinking aloud.

"I never thought about it that way. I would say that those who think like me have stood with the historical Judaic/Christian heritage." John said. "We did not change. Society did."

Lisa thought about it for a few moments. Then she challenged him. "You say you love Ben and his partner, but you can't accept who he is. Why can you not just accept that?" Lisa asked.

"I believe the Bible when it says that God created mankind in his own image, male and female. Everything about nature says that God only created two sexes: male and female."

"But you can't deny how people feel about themselves. If someone says they are gay, you've just got to accept it," Lisa said.

"No, I don't. I don't believe that's what God made anyone to be. But you confuse accepting this as normal with loving my son. I may not accept his behavior or self-identification, but I will always love him and affirm him as my son. Surely you can understand that?" John asked.

"I guess so," Lisa answered, but in truth she didn't. "By the way, are they married? It's legal you know," Lisa said.

"Yes, I know it's legal. And no, as far as I know they have never married. I assure you, Ben would tell me. He would probably call me and ask me to do the wedding just so that there would be another blow up between us," John said with frustration.

"Because you would refuse, right?" Lisa asked.

"That's right," John answered. "But I would attend the wedding," John added. "He is my son and I do love him."

"Does he know that?" Lisa asked.

"Yes," John said. "He's always known that, at least I think he does. I tell him every time we talk."

"How often do you talk?" she pressed.

"As often as Robert can make it happen," John said. "While Robert and I agree to disagree on the issue of homosexuality, we both share a love for Ben. He is my ally in trying to reconcile this relationship."

"Boy this is odd," Lisa said. "You don't accept homosexuality, but your son is gay. And your son's partner is your ally in trying to repair your relationship with your gay son."

"That's about the size of it," John said. "That's our family."

14

THE STORM

Lisa continued the conversation. "You still haven't told me why your time in the Senate was so short."

"No, I haven't," John said. He let out a deep sigh.

How could he tell her this part without prejudicing her against his sons? How could he explain what it was like to turn on the national news just a few weeks before Christmas and see his own son telling the world that his father, the Chaplain of the United States Senate, is a homophobe who would not accept his homosexuality and had disowned him?

On the day the storm began, John's assistant burst into John's office, picked up the TV remote from the credenza and pointed toward the flat panel screen hanging on the wall.

"You've got to see this," was all he said.

Suddenly John's youngest son Ben was on the screen with an *MSNBC* microphone in his face. They were somewhere on a sidewalk in San Francisco.

The graphic underneath Ben's image said, "Ben Grant, gay son of United States Senate Chaplain."

Ben was saying to the reporter, "...he did not accept the fact that I was gay. He couldn't. It's what he believes and what he has preached, all his life. We had harsh words and I left. I've never been back." Ben walked away from the camera. The reporter chased after him.

The reporter said, "So he kicked you out. Ben, did your father kick you out? Did he disown you?"

Ben stopped at the open back door of an SUV. He turned to the camera.

"Yeah, you might say that," he said. He climbed into the back of the SUV. As the camera operator shifted his position to get a view inside the vehicle you could see someone else. It was not his partner, Robert. It was his brother, Frank.

The reporter turned around to face the camera. "There you have it. The Chaplain of the United States Senate rejected and disowned his own gay son."

John was shocked beyond belief. He called Frankie. She had seen it, too. The phone at the office of the Senate Chaplain would not stop ringing. Members of the media wanted a statement. Would he and Frankie come on *CNN*, on *Fox*, on *Firing Line*, and so forth?

John left the Capitol to go back to the townhouse. A few members of the media waited outside, so he caught a cab rather than taking the subway. By five o'clock the media was camped outside the townhouse.

Frankie tried to call Ben immediately after seeing the news, but he would not answer or return the call. Later that evening Ben's partner, Robert, called John.

Robert said that he had no advance warning that Ben was going to do this. John assured him that what Ben said was not true. Robert said he believed him, but the damage was done.

John released a statement through the office of the chaplain saying the charges were not true. The Vice President expressed his support of John, as did other party leaders.

Congress went on recess for the holidays. They had planned to spend that first Christmas in D.C. as a family. Rachel, Frank, Cheryl, Jennifer and all the grandchildren were all coming. Not Ben, of course.

Two days after the story broke, Rachel arrived for the holidays and had to be ushered into the townhouse through the pack of hungry press hounds outside. Frank and Cheryl soon called saying they had a change of plans and were not coming. Jennifer also backed out at the last minute saying she couldn't stand the pressure. It was a lonely Christmas.

During the holidays the storm appeared to subside. Rachel returned to Africa a few days after the first of the year. John prepared for the return of Congress.

When Congress returned after the holiday break, hundreds of protestors were outside the Senate side of the Capitol demanding John's dismissal. John stepped to the podium to deliver the opening prayer of the first session, and over half of the members of the Senate turned their backs on him.

Chicago Tribune columnist Jerry Spraberry picked up on the story and wrote a savage hit piece on John. He indicted John as the leader of all fundamentalist Christian churches, declaring them out of step with the mainstream of Christianity. He also made a passionate call for the Senate to join the House in eliminating the office of chaplain.

"As a nation we have moved beyond the need for pious, religious bigots to give prayerful direction for Congress. It's time for the Senate to get in step with the march of progress and join the House. We no longer need congressional chaplains."

The day after the Spraberry column appeared, the minority party introduced a resolution to abolish the office of the Senate Chaplain. John was called to the Vice President's office along with the other leaders of the Senate. The majority leader said he could postpone consideration of the motion, but it had strong bi-partisan support. He could not prevent it. The resolution would pass.

It was decided that John should resign, but he was to wait until the President's Day recess in mid-February. In the meantime, guest ministers would be called on to do the prayer duties. John was to keep a low profile.

The press returned and camped outside the townhouse for weeks. Neither Frankie nor John could go anywhere. They were prisoners in a home they did not own. They had nowhere to go.

Lisa wondered if he had forgotten the question. His eyes were closed, and he seemed lost, like he had mentally gone to another world.

"Pastor John," she said softly.

John opened his eyes. "I'm sorry, what was it you asked?"

Lisa said, "Why was your stay in D.C. so short?"

John thought a moment. "Let's just say accusations were made that I was a narrow minded, bigoted homophobe, and those accusations would not go away. I became a political liability. I had to go."

"So," Lisa said, "you moved from a townhouse owned by that Troxell fellow to the high-tech house owned by that Troxell fellow."

"Not immediately," John said. "This is where Bob Burns comes into the picture."

"Oh, he so gives me the creeps," Lisa said. "You know sometimes he just shows up inside the house. I never hear a door chime or anything. He is just there." Lisa shuddered at the thought. "He's creepy."

"He has always done that, ever since we have been in the house. I think it's his way of reminding me that he is in control, just in case I know something," John said.

"Know something about what?" Lisa asked.

"Oh," John said, "about market manipulation and the National Strategic Petroleum Reserves. Just stuff like that."

15

THE SETUP

"Before all the controversy started, before Thanksgiving, the Vice President called to say he was sending a guy over to the townhouse and that we should listen to him," John said.

"About an hour later Bob Burns shows up. He was all business but seemed a nice enough guy. He gave us his card. He was an accountant in the capital city back home, but I had never heard of him before, which seemed strange. We pretty much knew everybody. He said he served a very small and exclusive client list that valued privacy. He told us that among that client list were some patriotic but anonymous people. They set up a trust fund to support us for as long as I was chaplain and even after I left the Senate."

"He said these patriots understood that we had served selflessly for many decades. Bob said we could turn over management of our financial resources to him if we wanted to, and these patriotic people would see to it that we had a more than adequate income for the rest of our lives. They would even take care of our future housing needs."

"We were understandably reluctant. He told us to take our time thinking about it. Then when everything blew up, we had nowhere to go. Bob said there was a house back home we could live in until we figured out what we wanted to do. Suddenly we were not in a position to say no. A few weeks after the President's Day recess, when the press was no longer watching, we moved out of D.C., and into the house."

"We started turning our financial life over to Bob. Not everything, mind you, and not all at once. His financial advice was excellent. We saw amazing returns. Then when Frankie got sick... we were trapped."

"So that's how you got tied up with that guy," Lisa said.

"That's how it happened," John said.

Lisa asked if John was getting hungry. He was. So they took the next exit where there was a *Cracker Barrel*. They enjoyed a nice lunch and walked around the shop a bit.

Back in the car, Lisa realized that what was to come next was the reason for all the secrecy. John was going to ask her to do something. She felt both nervous and excited. Nervous, because this was big-time stuff and she might not be able to do whatever John wanted her to do. Excited—well, she hadn't felt this alive in a long time. This was unbelievable.

John said that much of what he had told her he had never before told anyone. What he was going to tell her next was even more sensitive, things he had never told Frankie. He said he was counting on her complete confidence.

Lisa said he could count on her. Anyway, who would she tell?

John began telling her a story.

Washington is a town subject to gossip. It is a town that loves a scandal. It is a town that rarely disappoints.

In mid-November while John was Chaplain of the Senate, a large portion of the Strategic Petroleum Reserves quietly disappeared. Few noticed.

With Congress in the rush to take care of business and recess for the holidays, the issue couldn't gain any traction. Plus, the flood of oil into the market had driven gas prices down, just in time for the holidays. Everyone likes lower gas prices, and members of Congress were quick to stand up and try and take at least partial credit.

Just before the recess, a new issue came forward to divert attention away from the Strategic Petroleum Reserves—a homophobic Senate chaplain.

With the attention focused on John, nobody cared anymore about the decrease in petroleum reserves. Nobody noticed a drop in the value of certain oil stocks. And nobody noticed a quiet move from various sources to buy a controlling interest in Southern Oil, H. J. Troxell's biggest competitor in the oil business.

Almost no one.

Amber Cole, a financial analyst with the Washington Post, took note of some of this activity and wrote about it in a Sunday column. Then, after John's disastrous prayer on the opening day of the Senate after the holiday break, a leak to the *Washington Post* pointed a finger at Senator Joe Holloway.

Joe was a member of the Senate Energy and Natural Resources Committee and was also on the Energy Subcommittee. He had introduced legislation that fall that allowed for certain improvements at two of the four petroleum reserve sights near the gulf coast, one of those in his state. It seemed to be pretty routine legislation, part need and part pork.

Amber Cole pointed out that an amendment was attached to the bill at the last minute that allowed for the reduction of the Strategic Reserve levels without the President's approval under certain conditions.

The bill moved quickly through the Senate. It moved rapidly without changes through the House. President Tate signed it the day it arrived at his desk.

The bill allowed the Secretary of Energy to temporarily lower the reserves without the President's knowledge if a certain amount of repair work or improvements were being done at one or more of the four reserve sites. The bill created that very situation.

The market was flooded with cheap oil, driving down gas prices and affecting stock prices in the oil industry. About that time Joe Holloway's personal trust bought stock in Southern Oil at a very low price. Several weeks later, the trust sold it at an enormous profit. It looked like stock manipulation.

Amber Cole's second article in the Post made Joe look guilty. Quickly, finger-pointing began in the Senate. The minority blamed the majority for creating this dangerous situation for personal gain. The majority in the Senate pointed fingers at the majority in the House, where the parties were reversed in a split Congress.

FOX, *CNN*, *ABC*, *CBS*, and *NBC* were all asking what happened to the petroleum reserves and how had it happened. The President claimed no knowledge of the whole affair but acted quickly to cut off the flow of oil. Gas prices went up again, and so did stock prices. What was unseen was that through others, H. J. Troxell made millions in stock transactions and gained controlling interest of a competitor.

Joe denied any knowledge of the rider on his bill. Regardless, he was put up on ethics charges and was under investigation by the SEC for possible criminal charges. He could not claim ignorance of the trust fund transactions.

Joe came over to the townhouse the night after the story broke. John, still a virtual prisoner in the townhouse, was waiting for the President's Day recess so he could resign. Joe was distraught. He knew how serious these charges were.

He didn't look good.

John and Joe sat together in the basement study, two lifelong friends who had since childhood wanted to have a positive influence on the world. One was being wrongly accused of being a prejudiced homophobe, the other wrongly accused of criminal activity.

"I don't know what happened," Joe said. "That amendment got attached to my bill after we moved it out of the subcommittee."

"And the stock thing. An insurance guy I know suggested that the stock price on Southern Oil looked like a good opportunity. I investigated it, and he was right. So, I passed the information on to the trustee of my blind trust. He jumped in, big time. I had no idea what was going on, but nobody, I mean nobody, is going to believe me," Joe said forlornly.

"A month later demand for that stock was going through the ceiling. My trust made over $500,000 just like that," he said with a snap of his fingers. "They're going to crucify me, John, in the press. They will hang me out to dry, just like they have done to you.

"God, how did we get in this mess?" Joe dropped his head into his hands.

John walked across the room offering his longtime friend a glass of wine and a half-empty bottle. "I don't have anything stronger to offer you. You know that," he said.

Joe accepted the glass. "I'm surprised you have this," he said. He downed the wine and poured himself more.

"Drinking never makes a situation better," John said. He went back to his recliner.

"I believe God can bring good from all of this, Joe. We just have to have faith."

Joe shook his head. "I don't know, John. I'm not as sure about things as I once was. I don't have your faith."

"Don't say that Joe. Things will look different tomorrow," John sad.

Unfortunately, things did not. Three months after John and Frankie moved out of D.C., Joe suffered a massive stroke and died. John officiated his funeral at First Church. Vice President Simpson attended and stayed the night at the house with John and Frankie. Every news article about Senator Joe Holloway's death included paragraphs about the scandal.

16

THE REQUEST

John asked Lisa where they were.

"We're getting pretty close to Port St. Lucie, about 45 minutes," she said.

John pulled a piece of paper out of his pocket. "There's a *Sunoco* station just west of the Turnpike when we get off for SW Port St Lucie Boulevard," he said. "We need to go there. Mike and Jane will meet us, and we will swap out cars."

"Okay," Lisa responded. "This is so we will arrive at the condo in the minivan and go back in the minivan. Right?" she asked.

"Yes," John answered. "And Rachel will be going back with us. We will not be able to talk about this anymore after we swap vehicles. Anyway, I don't want Rachel to know about it. I need to ask you to do something for me."

Lisa thought to herself. "This is it, then. After all he has told me, now he is going to tell me what he wants me to do."

"What is it?" Lisa asked.

"I want you to find a former Senate Energy Subcommittee staffer named Jason Clarke. I believe he's responsible for the amendment that was added to Joe's energy bill. I believe at the time he was working for Troxell, or someone close to Troxell. I need you to convince him to go to the press and tell what really happened. I want to clear Joe Holloway's name."

"How do you know about this Clarke guy?" she asked.

"I can't tell you."

"But you're certain he's the one responsible?"

"I have good information on that."

"Okay. Where is he?" Lisa asked.

"I don't know."

"Do you have any clues?"

"My last information is that after leaving the Senate job he moved to Denver, Colorado," John said.

"And how old is that information?"

"Several years. It's all I've got. He would have been paid handsomely for his work, and Troxell stands to lose a lot if this guy goes public. I have plenty of money in my private account to pay for whatever you need. With Rachel home, I won't need you for a few weeks so no one will think anything about you not being around."

"What if it takes longer than that?" Lisa asked.

"We'll cross that bridge when we get there," John said. "Can I count on you?"

Lisa thought, "So this is all he wants? Find this guy, wherever he is, and ask him to go public about illegal activity and implicate one of the richest, most powerful men in the world."

Aloud she said, "Absolutely. Just tell me where to start."

17

THE ARRIVAL

After swapping vehicles at the *Sunoco* station, Lisa and John arrived at the St. James Golf Club condos where the wedding party was staying. It was just a few miles down Veterans Memorial Parkway from the Botanical Gardens where the wedding would take place. Mike and Jane took a little excursion to the beach and would arrive the next day at the condo.

Lisa went into the office to check in. A woman stood at the desk. She was about five foot nine, thin, with short sandy hair. She had a sharp nose, high cheekbones, and eyes that sparkled. It was Rachel. Though they had never met, they had talked on the phone and Lisa had seen many photos of her. She looked like her mother. Lisa would have recognized her anywhere.

"Rachel?" Lisa inquired. "I'm Lisa Smithy. I help your father. He is out in the van."

Rachel turned around, broke into a warm smile and quickly embraced Lisa.

"I am so glad to finally meet you," she said.

"I'm glad to finally meet you," Lisa responded.

"I can't thank you enough for all you do for my father. He really loves you," Rachel added.

Lisa said, "I do love him, and you, you look..." she hesitated. "You are beautiful, just like the photos of your mother," she said.

Rachel smiled, and her eyes glistened. "Thank you," she said. "But I could never be as beautiful as my mother," she added.

"But you are."

"Come on." Rachel continued. "Let's get Dad. I've got us checked in, and I've got the keys. We have a lot of catching up to do."

Rachel and Lisa headed out to the van where John was waiting. He was sitting there with his head down. A Carrie Underwood song was blasting over the van's stereo system.

Rachel opened the door. "Dad, since when did you start listening to country music?" Rachel said with an impish grin on her face.

John looked up. It was like looking at Frankie from years ago - that same playful smile, that same energy for living. It was the face of joy.

Rachel leaned in and gave her father a huge hug. Once he got his arms around her, he squeezed. Rachel was surprised at the strength of his squeeze. He wouldn't let her go for a moment. Then he looked into her eyes, and a vast, uncontrollable smile spread across his face.

He hung on to that gaze for several moments, letting his eyes soak up every bit of her. She looked so good, so alive.

He missed her so much.

"It's all Lisa's fault," he said. "She's corrupting me."

"Pastor John," Lisa said.

They laughed a bit, and Lisa wiped tears away from her eyes. She had not seen real happiness in Pastor John's eyes before now.

John, Rachel, and Lisa were sharing a first floor, handicap accessible three-bedroom condo. As Lisa and Rachel got the luggage, John slowly walked around with his cane checking things out. A huge fruit basket with a welcome card that had Olivia and Logan's name embossed on it adorned the center of the dining table. Also on the table was a schedule for the next few days and a list of who was staying in which condos.

John couldn't help but smile when he saw that Mike and Jane were sharing a three-bedroom condo with Bob Burns. There was a question mark by Bob's name like it was unclear if he was actually coming.

He would be there. John knew he would. After two days of hearing nothing but country music, Bob Burns would be snooping around to see what was going on.

A set of French doors opened to a covered patio, which overlooked the water and one of three golf courses that made up the luxury golf resort.

John was confident that Frank was out there somewhere playing golf with his buddies. He would never miss an opportunity to play golf. According to the schedule, all the family was to meet for dinner at 6:00 at a restaurant called Shuckers on the Beach.

John overheard Lisa and Rachel talking in the kitchen.

"Lisa, he really looks good," Rachel said. "I cannot thank you enough for how you have taken care of my father."

Lisa responded, "It's really not anything I've done. When he learned of the wedding, it energized him. Pastor John allowed the physical therapist to come back. He was determined to get strong enough for this trip."

"I'm not surprised. You're not supposed to have favorites, but Olivia was always special. She was their first grandchild. She spent more time with him and Mother than all the others grands combined," Rachel said.

"Well," Lisa said, "he looks better, and he is stronger, but the home healthcare nurse says we have to be careful."

"Josie?" Rachel said with raised eyebrows.

"Yes, Josie," Lisa responded with a smile. "I promised her that I would make him rest."

"Of course. Josie told me the same. But he is better now, and a large part of that is because of you!" She took both of Lisa's hands as she spoke.

Lisa looked down at the ground. She felt so blessed to be with Pastor John and to now be with Rachel. She looked up, and all she could say was, "Thank you."

They both decided that John should rest. So, after a piece of fruit and some catching up, John went to his bedroom and stretched out.

He closed his eyes and thought about their time in Washington.

~~~~~

They were in the townhouse, just a few days before he would resign from the Senate. The members of the press who had been parked out front on the street for weeks had finally left. It was late. It was cold. Frankie had already gone up to get ready for bed. John was setting up the coffee pot for her for in the morning.

His cell phone rang.

"Dr. Grant?"

"Yes."

"Please open the back gate. The Vice President of the United States wants to see you." It was the VP's Secret Service detail.

John hesitated. He had had enough of Vice President Jim Sessions. But, you don't say no to the Vice President of the United States.

"Okay," John answered. He hung up and went down the half flight of stairs to the back door that opened to the rear parking area. On the wall by the door was an intercom that was connected to the gate and a button that would open the back gate.

He pressed the button.

John looked out the window. Each of the townhouses on this block had parking spaces in the alley between the two rows of buildings. Plus, there were a few extra spaces and enough room to turn around. There was a security guard 24 hours a day. Any and all traffic in or out was logged.

It started to snow. A black SUV pulled into the small parking area. He could see outside the closing gate another black SUV that now blocked the entrance to the alley. John watched as two Secret Service agents came to the door.

John let them in and offered to take their coats. They refused.

"Dr. Grant, I'm Agent Carlisle; this is Agent Martin. We are with the Vice President's detail." They flashed their badges and ID cards. "Is there anyone else in the house with you?" he asked.

"Just my wife. She's upstairs in the master bedroom getting ready for bed," John answered.

"Would you go up ahead of me and warn her of my presence? Agent Martin will walk through this floor and the basement," he said.

John's face showed his displeasure at this intrusion. The agents were unmoved. "Certainly," he said. "This way."

John took Agent Carlisle around to the front stairway, and they started up. He called out as they climbed.

"Frankie, I've got a Secret Service agent with me. He needs to verify that we are the only people in the house."

A moment later Frankie appeared at the top of the stairs with her robe pulled tight around her body and a quizzical look on her face.

"The Vice President is here to see me," John said.

They stood together at the top of the stairs holding hands as Agent Carlisle invaded their private living space and completed a sweep of the top floor. He then moved down to the floor underneath.

After a moment Agent Martin called out from below, "All clear."

Agent Carlisle came back up the stairs to where John and Frankie stood. He said, "Dr. Grant, the Vice President would like to speak with you alone. Where is the best place for you to talk?"

John sighed, "In the basement. There's a study."

John and Frankie looked at one another, and she showed a sympathetic face toward the love of her life. He released Frankie's hand. John and the agent started down the stairs.

On the main level, they turned back toward the kitchen and then down the half flight to the back door. At the door they met Vice President Simpson with Agent Martin.

He removed his coat and handed it to Agent Martin. "John, thank you for seeing me this late. I need to talk to you, in private," the VP said.

John said, "Come on down to the basement. We can talk in the study."

They continued down the stairs to the basement level. Agent Carlisle followed but stayed outside the door when they entered the study. Sessions shut the door.

John thought about how just a few days ago he and Joe were down in the basement trying to figure out what to do about the mess he was in. Now, here was the Vice President.

"I don't have anything to offer you other than water," John said. He and Frankie did not normally drink alcohol, other than an occasional glass of wine. Joe had finished off the last bottle. He knew the VP drank heavily on occasions.

"I don't need anything," Simpson said. He looked like he desperately wanted a drink. "I need to be sure of something before we begin. Dr. Grant, as Chaplain of the Senate, you are my minister, correct?"

John thought for a minute. "You are a Catholic. I am a Protestant Minister. So I'm not your priest, but yes, as Chaplain of the Senate and you as a member of the Senate, I believe we enjoy that kind of a relationship," John answered.

"I need to know for certain that this is the nature of that relationship," Simpson pressed. "Right now as we speak, are we under the umbrella of the clergy/penitent relationship?"

"Why is that important?" John asked.

"Because I need to know that this conversation is confidential. If I were talking to my priest, he would be bound by his vows to keep our conversation private. Can I count on the same thing from you?"

"Yes," John answered. "But given the fact that you are Catholic wouldn't you rather be talking to your priest? This has the feeling of a confession, and I cannot offer absolution, at least not as your faith believes a priest can."

"No," the Vice President answered. "I need to talk to you, as my chaplain."

John looked at the Vice President of the United States. Dark circles surrounded his eyes. He looked as if he had the burden of the world on his shoulders. John was his chaplain, at least for a few more days. He had a moral and spiritual obligation.

"Okay, Mr. Vice President. You have my promise that whatever is said here tonight is confidential. Please, be seated," John said.

Simpson sat down. John pulled a chair over next to him. "What's on your mind?" John asked.

For the next thirty-five minutes, the Vice President of the United States unfolded a story that John could hardly believe.

John had been set up. His sons were involved. A lot of money was involved. Joe Holloway had been framed. A rich and powerful man named H. J. Troxell, who had been Simpson's most significant financial supporter, had done all of this to create a distraction.

The Vice President went into details. Troxell's people set up John's appointment as Chaplain. They knew John was vulnerable because of his relationship with his gay son and that with the proper handling this could become a hot issue.

John's son Frank had been paid off to set up the street interview with his brother Ben and the *MSNBC* reporter. Frank had also been given a lucrative job with one of Troxell's businesses in Florida as a reward for pulling it off.

A Senate committee staffer had been paid to add an amendment to Joe Holloway's bill. Members of the House who were in Troxell's pocket made sure the bill moved through the House without a problem. And the President was certain to sign the bill.

An insurance agent paid by Troxell spent months fostering a friendship with Joe just to plant the tip about the stock in Southern Oil.

Everything was timed to create a distraction to cover up what Troxell was really doing; manipulating the market to make a small fortune and taking over a competitor.

The Vice President claimed he didn't know about any of this in advance. When he interviewed John for the Chaplain's position, it was in good faith. But now that it was all over, there wasn't anything he could do about it. He couldn't go public because it would ruin his career and possibly bring down the President. With the terrorist threat in the world and the current troubles in the Middle East and Europe, there was too much at stake. What was done was done.

"I've come to really like you and your wife," Simpson said. "And you know, Joe has been one of my best friends. I feel bad about all of this, and I hope you will forgive me. I hope Joe will forgive me." He paused and looked down. "I hope God will forgive me."

The Vice President stood up to leave.

John said, "Wait a minute, sir. What are you looking for here? Are you expecting some kind of absolution from me? Because if you are, I don't give it. I can't give it."

"Dr. Grant," Simpson said, "I'm not sure what I am expecting here. I just had to get this off my chest. In the short time I have known you..." He paused, looking for the right words.

"You came up here expecting to do something good, something special. You had great ideas. You were used, and now you are being discarded. We do this to one another around here almost without remorse. Those of us who have been here for a long time, we come to expect it. Truth is we deserve it. You and your wife did not. You are a good and decent man.

"I'm sorry."

The Vice President turned and opened the door. Agent Carlisle still stood at his post. They went up the stairs to the back of the townhouse. Agent Martin helped him put on his coat, and out the back door they went.

John followed just a few steps behind. Frankie was standing in the kitchen with a glass of water. She joined John at the back door. They watched the black SUV turn around and exit through the security gate. It was snowing harder. The SUV left tracks.

Frankie looked at her husband. "John, what was that all about?"

All John could say was, "I can't tell you." His voice shook with anger.

~~~~~

"Pastor? Pastor?" Lisa shook his arm.

John blinked his eyes. Where was he? For a few moments he was confused. The surroundings were not familiar. Then it all came back to him. He was in a condo in Florida. He was here for Olivia's wedding. Rachel was here.

He had been dreaming.

"It's time to get ready to meet everyone for dinner," Lisa said.

18

THE FAMILY

Lisa and Rachel decided that John should use the wheelchair that night. The next couple of days would be taxing, at best. It would be easier and quicker to get in and out of the restaurant using the wheelchair.

John didn't like it, but he didn't argue. The truth was that he was eager to see his grandchildren and hungry for seafood.

It was only about a 10-minute drive to the resort where Shuckers was located. At the entrance a half-buried skiff with a sign made of drift wood draped with fishing net announced with bright letters, "Shuckers on the Beach." A marque welcomed the families of Olivia and Logan. Their private room, located in the back with a free bar, had a row of tables in the shape of a "T." A set of large windows overlooked the beach and the crystal blue Atlantic.

Frank stood at the bar with a drink in hand. Jennifer stood with him, along with Logan's mother and stepfather. On the other side of the room stood Jim and Carol, Jennifer's two children.

Jim saw them first.

"Aunt Rachel!" he called out. Jim was tall and slender, a handsome young man with light hair and intense eyes. He hurried across the room to greet them.

"Jim," Rachel practically screamed. "Oh, I hardly recognized you. Look at you."

They embraced.

"Have you gotten a job?" she asked.

"Yes, I finished my master's in international banking in December. I'm now working for a German bank with offices in Houston," Jim answered.

Jim loved his Aunt Rachel. When his mother and father split up, it was Aunt Rachel who came and got Jennifer out of bed and on with life. Jim had to assume leadership for the family because his mother never entirely got back on her feet. She seethed resentment and was at times pitifully dependent. But at other times, when it suited her, she could be charming and resourceful. Whenever things were terrible with his mother, he could always call on Aunt Rachel, and she would know what to do.

"Now tell me, Jim, have you got a girlfriend?" Rachel asked. "You're a great catch."

Jim grinned and flushed just a bit. "Well, I did meet a girl recently. It's not anything, yet. But..." He looked down and shuffled his feet. "You never know," he said with a twinkle in his eye. "She might be the one."

Rachel said, "Okay, you absolutely have to tell me all about her."

"Not before he speaks to me," John said as he rolled his chair over. "Jim, how's my man?" John said.

"Granddad!" Jim held out his hand. Jim bent over, and they embraced. They had always been close. "How's the new job, hotshot?" John asked.

"It's great, Granddad. This is a great company. I'm learning a lot. I really like it," he said.

Jennifer walked over. "Daddy, I'm glad to see you." She bent over and hugged him dutifully. "I didn't expect you to be in a wheelchair," she said. As she said that, she looked up at Lisa with an accusatory look.

John responded, "Oh, don't let this fool you. I'm fit as a fiddle. This was Rachel and Lisa's idea. They don't want me to overdo it."

Lisa extended her hand. "Hi. I'm Lisa Smithy, your father's helper," she said.

Jennifer did not return her hand.

"I'm sorry," John said. "I should have done introductions. Everyone, everyone," he spoke loudly and got the attention of everyone in the room. "This is Lisa Smithy. She helps me. She's the reason I'm able to be here today."

Jim shook her hand. Carol, Jim's younger sister, came across the room and introduced herself. She had flowing blond hair and blue eyes, sporting an attractive pant suit outfit.

Frank, along with Logan's parents, started across the room toward her.

Jennifer said, "I didn't think the help was invited," as she turned around and walked away.

Lisa thought to herself, "How rude."

Frank stepped up with glass in hand, bent forward and lightly kissed Lisa on the cheek. "So glad to finally meet you. I've heard so much about you."

He was already on his way to being drunk.

Logan's mother extended her hand. "Hi, I'm Susan Street, and this is my husband, Phil."

Phil extended his hand. "We're so glad to meet you."

Susan spoke with a toothy smile, and her salt and pepper hair bounced. Nearly bald, Phil stood a good two inches shorter than Susan. They were dressed casually.

Lisa said, "I'm happy to meet you, Congratulations. I know you are proud." It was awkward.

Rachel stepped up beside Lisa as introductions were made.

There was a commotion behind them. Logan and Olivia had arrived. Olivia was immediately hugging John while Susan made a fuss over her sundress and shoes.

As everyone gathered around Olivia and Logan, Rachel pulled Lisa aside and whispered. "You need to have your armor on tonight, girlfriend. But don't worry, I've got your back."

Lisa worked her way to the table and put her purse down, marking a spot for her and Rachel. She removed a chair between them so Pastor John could roll right up to the table in his chair.

Suddenly someone had her by the arm and was dragging her toward the bar. It was Frank.

Frank looked exactly like what he was; a middle-aged, balding man trying not to look middle-aged, who drank too much. He wore baggy khakis. A loose-fitting, open collared blue shirt revealed gray chest hairs. His gaudy gold chains hung from a nearly invisible neck.

"Come on, Lisa," he said. "Let's get you properly lubricated for this evening's festivities."

"Uh, well," she tried to protest. They arrived at the bar. "Actually, I don't drink," Lisa said apologetically.

"Well, of course you drink. Everybody drinks, except my father. Come one, what's your poison?" Frank persisted.

Lisa looked around the room, looking for a rescue, something, someone. She said, "I don't see your wife here, do I? Her name is Cheryl, right?"

"No, she's not here. And she won't be, either," he said with a wink.

Still looking for a way out, she decided to talk about his wife. "Oh, is she ill? I hope not. Is she all right? I enjoyed talking to her on the phone," Lisa blurted out in rapid-fire sequence.

"Don't you lie now. Nobody, I mean nobody, enjoys talking to Cheryl on the phone. She's not here. She's... busy, taking care of wedding decorations and stuff." Frank took the final gulp from his glass, handed it to the bartender and said, "Fill it again."

Lisa saw Rachel headed her way. Rescue was coming.

Frank carried on. "You're a very attractive woman. I'm glad old dad brought you along to liven up this party. Come on now, what do you have?"

Frank grabbed her arm tighter and pulled her closer. He was hitting on her!

Rachel arrived, "Come on Frank. Give poor Lisa a break. She's here to help your dad, not to drink with you." Rachel pulled Lisa away from Frank's grasp.

"That doesn't mean she can't have a good time," he said, with a slur in his speech, his arms spread like, what gives!

As Rachel pulled Lisa away, Frank smacked her on the bottom. Lisa turned around ready to slap his face, but she thought better of it. Rachel stepped between them.

Rachel got right up into her brother's face. "Frank, that was highly inappropriate!" she said firmly. "But typical," she said to Lisa as she walked her to the table.

Frank said as they moved away, "Thank you, Saint Rachel. You've saved the day, again." He raised his freshly filled glass in the air.

Rachel whispered to Lisa as they made their way to their place at the table. "The fun has begun."

Lisa noticed some other young adults had joined the crowd. Rachel pointed out Frank's sons, Jacob and Cole. Cole was a student at Florida State, and Jacob was, well, he was Jacob. She didn't know what he did.

Lisa knew what he did, based on what Pastor John had told her. He looked like a druggy. Cole, on the other hand, looked like a nice young man. He was talking to Pastor John.

Logan and Olivia came to the center of the table. Logan had an earring in his left year and tattoos on both arms. He was wearing a loose white cotton shirt with baggy khaki shorts. They were clean and pressed. His hair was short and spiked, and he sported a thin, neatly trimmed beard. He ran his own pool service, which explained the deep tan.

Olivia wore a white sundress that was gathered at the top and loose from the waist down to mid-calf. She sported a pair of spiked sandals, Neiman Marcus, she had told her future mother-in-law. Her bleached blond hair billowed over her shoulders. She had a beautiful tan and was very attractive. Rachel told Lisa that Olivia was a lawyer with a large area law firm. They already had a condo in the West Palm Beach area.

Lisa was suddenly aware of how pale she was compared to all these Floridians.

Frank came to the table, picked up a spoon and tapped his glass. Everyone got quiet.

"We are here to begin the celebration of the marriage of these two beautiful people—Logan and Olivia!" His speech was slurred even more.

Everyone clapped and moved toward the table. Cole rolled John to his place between Rachel and Lisa. Jennifer came up and bumped Lisa. Her intent was obvious. She wanted Lisa to move down a seat so that Jennifer could be seated next to her father.

Lisa picked up her purse; Carol was in the next seat. Jim was across from her. The last one was open. Then Jacob, Frank's older son, came and claimed the seat directly across from Lisa.

"Great," Lisa thought. "I get to sit across from the druggy."

19

THE TOAST

The food was fabulous. John had oysters on the half shell with grilled grouper. Lisa had grilled salmon with steamed vegetables. Rachel had shrimp alfredo with a salad.

They were just about the only ones not drinking alcohol. Frank, at the head of the table, was drunk and getting drunker. Sitting across from Lisa, Jacob was downing one beer after another. Carol, Jennifer's youngest child, had wine, but only took sips. She was sober.

Lisa enjoyed talking with Carol. She was working on her master's degree in social work at Texas A&M. She was also in a serious relationship with a young man from Mississippi, an engineering grad student. They were both active in a church in College Station called The Brazos Fellowship.

Their conversation was continually interrupted by obnoxious comments from an increasingly drunk Jacob. They were obviously not close as cousins.

Across from Carol sat Cole, Jacob's brother. He was polite and a bit reserved. He also was not drinking. He would apologize and make excuses for his brother, and several times told Jacob to just keep quiet.

It certainly was not a dull evening, Lisa had to say.

As is often the case when families gather, the same old stories were told. Rachel told how she and Jennifer got locked in the upstairs bathroom one time and the fire department came, put up a tall ladder and a fireman climbed through the window to get them out.

Jennifer reminded everyone of the Christmas when Santa's gifts got locked in a storage room at the church and Daddy didn't have the right key. Trying to break into the room he set off the alarm and the police came and tried to arrest him.

"It's true," John said, holding up his arms like he was surrendering. "It's true. I was handcuffed in my own church on Christmas Eve."

Susan, Logan's mother, told that as a little boy, he was afraid of Santa Claus. As a result, they never got a decent photo of Logan in Santa's lap because he was always screaming.

Everyone laughed. Logan said, "Hey, a fat guy in a red suit with a fake beard? What's not to be afraid of?"

"That's nothing," Jacob chimed in from the other end of the table. "Tell 'em, Frank. Tell 'em how you shot the Easter Bunny."

Everyone looked toward Frank, who was laughing so hard he couldn't talk. Rachel finally chimed in.

"It was Easter Sunday morning. Dad was up really early, before dawn for some reason. He was outside hiding Easter eggs so that when we got up, we could have an Easter egg hunt before going to church. Frank heard the noise and opened his second story window. He saw someone in the bush below and started shooting at him with his BB gun."

"And I got him too, right in the ass!" Frank said too loudly.

Everyone was laughing.

John added. "That afternoon, after conducting three services that morning, I had to go to the emergency room and have BBs removed from my backside. I couldn't sit for a week." Everyone roared.

Then Jim, Jennifer's son, said, "Mom, tell them about Uncle Ben and the box."

The whole family laughed, remembering that event. Jennifer finally said, "Well, it wasn't funny at the time. Frank told Ben that if he got inside a cardboard box, he could jump out the second-floor window and he would fly down to the patio unhurt. Ben, of course, believed him. He was only four, maybe five years old. He managed to get the window open and knock the screen off. He balanced the box on the window sill, climbed up in a chair and tried to get in.

"Mother walked up just as he went out the window. She screamed and ran down the stairs. Ben was sprawled out on the patio moaning. Frank came running up and saw Ben and the box and started crying, 'I've killed him, I've killed him, I've killed my brother.'"

"Mother was in a panic. She began checking Ben over. Later she realized the box hit one of the bushes and Ben landed in the box, which broke his fall. Then he tumbled out on the patio."

"Other than a few scrapes and having the wind knocked out of him, Ben was okay. But I thought Mother was going to kill Frank," Jennifer finished.

Then Frank said, "We would have been better off if the little faggot had died."

It got quiet around the table really fast.

"Daddy," Olivia said.

John decided it was time to change the subject. He moved the wheelchair back slightly, locked it down and then stood up. Rachel stood to help him, but he really didn't need the help. He cleared his throat. He obviously wanted to say something.

Frank muttered, "Oh boy, here it comes."

"Daddy!" Olivia stared at her father.

John raised his tea glass. "Though this is only sweet tea, I raise my sweet tea to the sweet and beautiful young lady at the center of the table, my Olive Oil."

Olivia turned from glaring at her father to smiling at her grandfather.

"You have brought delight and joy to this family since the day you were born. I only wish your grandmother were here to see what a beautiful and successful young woman you have become. Somewhere, she is looking, and she is pleased.

"And to you, Logan. You are one lucky guy."

"That I am, sir," Logan said.

Everyone murmured in agreement.

John continued. "Thank you, Susan and Phil, for raising such a fine young man to become a partner with my Olive Oil. To Olivia and Logan!"

Glasses were raised around the table. "To Olivia and Logan," they all said.

"Now, there is one other thing I want to say."

Frank grumbled at the end of the table. "This is it. It's sermon time."

Olivia glared at her father again.

John delayed for just a moment.

"I want to encourage you to make faith in God a partner in your marriage," John began.

Frank stood up. "Nobody cares anymore about your religious stuff, Dad," he said with slurred speech before slipping and falling onto the table, spilling drinks and knocking plates of food on them and onto the floor. Someone screamed. Susan and Phil jumped back from the table as alcohol and food splattered on them and around them.

Jennifer yelled at Frank to just shut the hell up. Jacob yelled at Jennifer to leave his father alone. Several others chimed in yelling at one another until Rachel thundered, "That's enough!"

Everyone got quiet. Olivia's face was streaked with tears. Logan's parents were covered in food and drink.

"We are not going to act this way," Rachel ordered. "Frank, you've had way too much to drink. Let's just call it a night."

With that, she turned to Lisa and said, "Help me."

They got a visibly shaken John back down into his wheelchair and started to the car. Lisa was shocked.

Rachel said, "I'm sorry you witnessed all of that. Family is hard."

20

THE DOCTOR

John was so upset he was physically ill. Before they could get him into the van, he threw up. Lisa could touch his chest and feel that his heart was racing and was out of rhythm. He was sweating profusely.

Jennifer followed them out. "Daddy, you're going to be alright. You're going to be alright," she said over and over. As Lisa and Rachel lifted him out of the chair and into the front passenger seat of the van, Jennifer tried to push Lisa out of the way.

"He's my father," she said.

"Jennifer," Rachel said firmly. "Let Lisa do her job."

With that, Jennifer backed off. She started crying even more.

As Rachel fixed John's seatbelt, Lisa turned to Jennifer and said, "Why don't you climb in and ride with us? We'll need your help getting him out and into his room."

Jennifer mumbled a tearful thank you.

As Lisa climbed into the driver's seat, Rachel gave her a look, like "why did you do that?" Lisa shrugged her shoulders. She felt sorry for Jennifer.

Rachel thought to herself, "That is what Jennifer wants. She wants everyone to feel sorry for her."

Lisa cranked the van just as Logan and Olivia ran up. She rolled down the window.

"Is Granddaddy going to be okay? Is he alright?" she asked with a worried expression on her tear-streaked face.

Lisa said, "I think he is just emotionally worn out. It was a long trip down. He needs to rest."

Lisa was lying. She was worried about Pastor John. She thought they should find the nearest hospital.

From the back, Rachel said softly but firmly, "Let's go!"

Lisa put the van in gear and backed out of the handicapped parking spot. As she drove away, she saw the rest of the family gather around Logan and Olivia.

Rachel had reclined John's seat before fastening his seat belt. Lisa didn't think he had lost consciousness, but he was not entirely with them either. He was making a strange sound.

Then he started weeping. The weeping grew stronger and stronger. It was like years of grief and worry about his family came pouring out.

Rachel and Jennifer both reached up from the second seat to touch and comfort their father. They wept with him.

Lisa had a hard time seeing to drive because of the tears that flooded her eyes. She reached down into her purse for a Kleenex. Then she remembered the instructions.

"Rachel," she said.

"Yes," Rachel answered as she wiped the tears from her eyes.

"I just remembered, before we left, Bob Burns gave me an emergency contact number for a doctor," she said.

Lisa handed her purse back to Rachel. "There is an envelope in the side pocket. It has the number. Maybe we should call the doctor."

"That's a good idea," Rachel said as she found the envelope. She turned on the overhead reading lamp and pulled a sheet of paper from the envelope. It was on stationary from Bob Burns' office. It listed a number for the medical service of Doctor Jordash Nordia.

Rachel called the service on Lisa's cell phone.

"Medical Services," a Cuban accented voice answered. "How may I help you?"

"Hello, my name is Rachel Grant. My father, Dr. John Grant, is ill. We were given this number to call while we are here in case he needed medical assistance. Can you help us?" she said.

"Can you give me the seven-digit code on the card you have?" the operator asked.

Rachel looked back in the envelope. There was a card. Highlighted on the front right of the card was a seven-digit code.

"Yes," she said. "I found it. It is 4783261."

The answering service operator typed the code into her computer. Immediately a notice came up on the screen indicating this was a top priority client and to inform Mr. Bob Burns of any contact with this client.

"Okay, Ms. Grant. I can send the doctor to see you. Can you describe the nature of the problem?" she asked.

"Okay, well, my father has had an emotional shock, I guess you could say. He has been through a really emotionally trying experience and has been crying uncontrollably," Rachel said.

Lisa chimed in. "Tell them his heartbeat is irregular and that he is on Tambocor, an ACE inhibitor, and a diuretic. He also takes a blood thinner because of a stroke and Lisinopril for his blood pressure."

Jennifer started crying again. "Daddy is on all those drugs?"

Rachel and Lisa both looked at her. Lisa thought to herself, "I should have left her back at the restaurant."

Rachel started repeating all that Lisa said when the operator on the line said, "I have his medical records before me. Are you staying at 102 St. James Golf Club resorts?"

"Yes. That's where we are staying," Rachel said. "Right now, we are in a van on our way back to the condo. We will be there in less than five minutes."

"Do you feel he is in imminent danger?" the operator asked.

"No, I don't think so," Rachel answered.

"Okay, then I will have the doctor meet you at the condo within the hour. Is there anything else I can do for you, Ms. Grant?" she asked.

Rachel was amazed. She knew her father didn't trust Bob Burns, but he sure knew how to take care of things. "No, I don't think so. Thank you very much," she said.

The operator replied, "If his condition should suddenly worsen you should go to the nearest emergency room or dial 911. Thank you for calling Medical Services."

With that, she hung up.

Rachel looked at the phone.

"What did she say?" Lisa asked.

"She said the Doctor will meet us at the condo within the hour. If his condition worsens we should call 911 or go to an emergency room," Rachel repeated what the operator had said.

Lisa raced down Veterans Memorial Boulevard toward the golf resort.

The Medical Service operator dailed the number for Bob Burns. High in the air over North Florida in a Gulf Stream 650, Bob was awakened by his phone.

"Bob Burns," he said.

When the trip down to Port St. Lucie had produced nothing but country music, Bob had become suspicious. Over a year ago he had two guys break-in to Mike and Jane Summers' house and copy their credit card numbers. These guys were good. They left no tracks, no evidence.

Mike and John had been spending a lot of time together. Bob had no evidence that John told Mike anything. Bob didn't even know if John knew anything. He knew about the Vice President's late-night visit years ago when John and Frankie were still in D.C. The guard at the gate logged the entry. But he had no idea what they had talked about that night. Mr. Troxell would not allow the townhouse to be bugged.

Bob was paid to be suspicious. He decided to keep a closer watch on Mike and Jane Summers. When he saw the charge on their Master Card for the SUV rental, he was curious. When he saw charges for the same hotel where John and Lisa had stayed on the same night, and for another for a hotel at Juno Beach for tonight, his interest was aroused.

He immediately called for the Gulf Stream. He would arrive at West Palm Beach International Airport before 10 PM. He would stay in a Troxell owned condo overnight and drive a rental to the condo on Friday afternoon like he had driven down to be part of the family celebration.

The operator said, "We have had a call for medical services for Dr. John A. Grant."

"What was the nature of the problem?" Bob asked.

"Apparently Dr. Grant has been through some emotional trauma, and his heart is out of rhythm. I am sending Dr. Nordia to the condo at 102 St. James Golf Resorts," the operator reported.

Bob thought for a minute. He had been babysitting this pastor for years, and he was tired of it. The call from the Medical Service gave him hope that maybe it all would end soon.

"Have Doctor Nordia call me before he arrives at the condo," he said.

"Yes sir," the operator replied.

Bob pressed the disconnect button on his phone. This was the opportunity he had been looking for.

Dr. Jordash Nordia was of Jamaican/American descent. He was a graduate of the St. George University School of Medicine on the Island of Grenada. This is the same medical school that was liberated by U.S. Rangers in the Invasion of Grenada in the 1980s.

Then President Ronald Reagan sent the U.S. Army in after a coup deposed of the ruling government and instituted a dictatorship. The victory took only a few weeks, and the liberated American medical students were allowed to complete their medical training in the United States. However, the Caribbean students had to stay and finish their training in Grenada.

The Caribbean medical school was often a stop of last resort for American students who could not get accepted in an American school. The Caribbean students who remained resented the Americans. None more than Dr. Jordash Nordia.

Now over 70 years old, Dr. Nordia had been practicing medicine in the Miami area for 30 years. His was a unique practice. All of his patients were from among the rich, jet set of the Miami area. Plus, a very special client of his was H. J. Troxell.

Dr. Nordia could be counted on to provide various prescriptions for the many needs of both friends and enemies of this powerful man. Tonight would be no different.

After about ten minutes Bob's cell phone rang again.

"Mr. Burns, Dr. Nordia here. How may I help you?"

"Jordash," Bob said, "we are in need of your special services tonight. This is a problem that needs to quietly," he paused a moment, "go away."

"I understand," Dr. Nordia said.

21

THE SHOT

Upon arriving at the condo, Lisa, Rachel, and Jennifer moved John into the wheelchair and to his bedroom. They partially undressed him and placed him in the bed. Rachel got a damp washcloth and began wiping his face.

He was conscious and still crying, but not the uncontrollable sobbing as earlier. He kept saying over and over, "I'm sorry. I'm so sorry. I did the best I could do."

"It's okay Daddy," Jennifer said. "You're the best father anyone could ever have."

"You can't blame yourself, Daddy. We love you," Rachel said.

Jennifer and Rachel sat on either side of the bed holding John's hands, softly encouraging and comforting him. Lisa placed her hand on John's chest. His racing heart had slowed down. She could not feel an irregular beat. The doctor might still hear it with his stethoscope, though.

The doorbell rang.

Lisa opened the door to a tall man dressed in a black tie-less suit. He had silver hair and a sharp beard with silver streaks and was carrying a medical bag. Behind him, in the parking lot, was a white Escalade whose driver stood at the rear door.

"I'm Dr. Nordia," he said with a heavy Caribbean accent.

"Oh, thank you, doctor, for coming so quickly. I'm Lisa, Pastor John's caretaker," Lisa said.

"So, Dr. Grant is a pastor?" Dr. Nordia asked.

"Yes. He's 72, retired, and is here for his granddaughter's wedding on Saturday," she said.

"I see," the Doctor said. "May I examine him?"

"This way." Lisa showed him to John's room. Rachel stood to greet him. Jennifer continued to hold John's hand.

"I'm his daughter Rachel; this is my sister, Jennifer," Rachel said.

"I'm Dr. Nordia," he said. He shook Rachel's hand and nodded toward Jennifer. Then he walked to the side of the bed and sat in the chair Rachel had been using. He touched John's forehead, then he reached into his bag and pulled out a stethoscope.

For several moments the doctor listened to John's heart. He moved the stethoscope to different positions on his chest, listening to his lungs.

"Help me," he said to Jennifer as he lifted John to a sitting position. He lifted John's t-shirt and listened to his lungs from the back.

After a few moments, he helped John back down. John was finally quiet. The doctor opened John's eyelids and shined a light on each pupil from a small flashlight he produced from an inside coat pocket. He reached into his bag and removed an automatic blood pressure device, which the doctor attached to John's wrist. Pressing a button, it began to inflate.

Then he reached back into the bag and pulled out a tongue depressor. Pulling down on John's chin, the doctor opened his mouth, suppressed the tongue and used the flashlight to look into John's open mouth.

The device beeped. He looked around for a trash can, saw one beside the bed table, and disposed of the tongue depressor. He put the small flashlight back into his inside coat pocket and retrieved a small pad and a pen. Dr. Nordia wrote down the blood pressure and pulse rate numbers that flashed on the front of the device. Then he leaned over and spoke to John.

"Dr. Grant? Dr. Grant? I'm Dr. Nordia. Can you hear me?"

John didn't respond.

The doctor repeated himself.

"Dr. Grant! Dr. Grant. I'm Dr. Nordia. Can you hear me?"

This time John turned his eyes toward the doctor. His eyes were still full of tears.

Dr. Nordia leaned back in the chair and rubbed his beard. "He has obviously been through something emotionally traumatic. He's in a state of shock. I clearly hear his defective mitral value.

He produced a small laptop from his bag, lifted the screen and touched the pad that read his fingerprint. The screen came alive. "I have his medical history. On the way over I studied it. Are there any additional medications besides the ones on his chart?"

"No," Lisa said. "But he did throw up as we were leaving the restaurant. I had given him his afternoon meds just before he ate. He has not had his evening meds."

"Okay," Dr. Nordia said. "He won't need his evening meds. I want to give him a sedative to help calm him down and relieve some of his emotional distress. I would also like to give him something to help him sleep."

Lisa looked concerned. She asked, "Can you tell me what you are giving him?"

Dr. Nordia stood and retrieved a pill packet, a vial containing some kind of drug, along with a syringe. He tore open the end of the pill packet and placed it on the bed.

"Are you a nurse?" he asked Lisa.

"No," Lisa answered. "But I am responsible for administering his meds. I would like to know what he is receiving."

"Nothing more than what he needs," the doctor responded. As he spoke, he picked up the syringe and uncovered the needle. He pushed the needle into the vial and held it up while he pulled the syringe plunger back, drawing the liquid into the body of the syringe. "Please, I need a glass of water."

Rachel and Lisa looked at one another. Rachel realized that Lisa was not leaving John's side, not until she knew what kind of medication he was being administered. Rachel headed to the kitchen for a glass of water.

"I would still like to know what you are giving him," Lisa said as she stepped between the doctor and John.

"I would like for you to step aside while I take care of my patient," Dr. Nordia said, as he thumped the side of the syringe, forcing any air bubbles to the surface.

Lisa stood her ground. Rachel returned with the glass of water.

Jennifer stood up and said, "Lisa, get out of the doctor's way."

"Not until he tells me what he going to administer to Pastor John," she said firmly.

Dr. Nordia stood to his full six foot one-inch height, and with a commanding voice said, "I need you to get out of my way."

"No," Lisa said.

"Move, Lisa," Jennifer ordered. "Get out of his way."

Dr. Nordia made a move toward John. Lisa drew in closer until she was touching the bed, blocking the doctor's way. "I want to know what that pill is and what is in that syringe!" she demanded.

"I am a doctor, and he is my patient. You are just hired help. You will move out of my way while I treat my patient!" he said with a rising and firm tone.

Lisa felt tears sting her eyes. It was the second time tonight she had been referred to as the "hired help." Her resolve did not soften.

"No," she said firmly. She stiffened her stand and tried to figure out what she would do if he decided to physically move her.

At that point, Rachel put the glass down and stepped to Lisa's side.

"I am not the hired help," Rachel said. "This is my father, and I demand to know what drugs you are trying to give him."

"Rachel!" Jennifer blurted out.

They all looked at one another. It was an impasse. Dr. Nordia was trying to determine his next move when John spoke.

"Jennifer, darling, would you go and get my Bible? I believe it is on the dining room table," he said softly.

They all looked down at John. He sat himself up on his elbows. His eyes were red from all the tears but his voice, though soft, was strong.

"Doctor," he said. "Thank you for coming out tonight. I appreciate your willingness to help, but the medicine I need tonight comes from the Great Physician."

Dr. Nordia looked at John, then at Lisa, Rachel, and Jennifer. Jennifer looked back at her father, and he repeated to her, "Go on, get my Bible."

Jennifer threw up her hands and left the room.

"I don't think we require your services anymore tonight," John said to the doctor.

Dr. Nordia paused a moment. He turned, picked up the cover and slid it back on the needle. Then he placed the syringe, the pill, and the vial back in his bag. He closed his small laptop and slid it into the pocket on the side. He zipped up the bag, turned back to them and said, "I'm glad he is better. Good night."

With that, Dr. Nordia turned and headed out toward the front door. At the door he met Carol and Jim, Jennifer's children, coming in.

"Is Granddad alright?" Carol asked her mother, who was returning with John's Bible from the dining room.

"I don't know what's going on," Jennifer snarled. "That was the doctor, and he's leaving. Lisa wouldn't allow him to give Daddy a shot."

Jim and Carol followed their mother into John's bedroom.

"Are you going to be okay, Granddad?" Jim asked. He looked at Lisa, "You wouldn't let the doctor give Granddad a shot?"

Rachel said, "It's okay Jim; please understand."

"I was in the room, and I don't understand," Jennifer said. "What is going on here?" she asked Lisa.

Lisa stood silently for a moment. "I didn't trust him," she finally said.

Rachel added, "He never did say what that pill was or what was in the syringe."

John broke in. "I didn't need his help. I'm going to be just fine." Then he turned to Jennifer. "Jennifer, would you find Psalm 18 in my Bible, please?"

"Okay, Daddy." Jennifer opened John's Bible. It was worn from years of use. Throughout its pages were underlined passages, and notes filled in the margins. Jennifer quickly found the passage.

"I've got it, Daddy," she said. She moved to hand the Bible to him, but he held up his hand.

"Read the first three verses of that chapter," he said.

Jennifer cleared her throat, then she read:

I love You, O Lord, my strength.
The Lord is my rock and my fortress and my deliverer,
My God, my rock, in whom I take refuge;
My shield and the horn of my salvation, my stronghold.
I call upon the Lord, who is worthy to be praised,
And I am saved from my enemies."

"Thank you, Jennifer," he said. "I'm going to be just fine… thanks to all of you." He looked around the room, then reached up and grabbed hold of Lisa's hand. Rachel took Lisa's other hand and reached for Jim's hand. Jim reached out for Carol's hand, and Carol reached for her mother's hand.

Jennifer put her father's Bible down on the bed, took Carol's hand and then took her father's other hand.

They all held hands, an unbroken circle.

"Say a prayer for us, Sport," John said to his grandson Jim.

"Sure, Granddad."

They all bowed their heads, and Jim prayed, "Dear God, thank you for Grandfather. Thank you for the example he and Grandmother gave us all our lives. Forgive us our sins this night. Help us to be as forgiving to others as you have been to us. Bless Olivia and Logan's wedding day. And help us all to behave. Amen."

And they all said in unison, "Amen."

22

THE FRIENDSHIP

Later, after John had taken his evening meds and settled into sleep, Lisa walked into the dining area. Jennifer sat there alone. Her father's Bible was open on the table before her.

Jennifer had the same attractive features common to her family, but she hid them with a poor haircut and too much makeup. She was the kind of woman who would easily fade unnoticed into the back ground. That life had been unkind to her was written all over her. Yet, she had an attractive smile and warm, dark eyes.

"I have to tell you how wonderful your children are," Lisa said. "I had the best time talking with them tonight before everything happened. Jim is such a gentleman, and Carol is a beautiful young lady. They are both smart and capable. They are two fine young people."

Jennifer looked at Lisa. "Thank you," she said. "I am proud of them."

Though Jennifer was about ten years older than Lisa, she realized that Lisa was more world-wise. Lisa had been through a lot but somehow had managed to do more than just survive. She found a way to thrive. She seemed to be a genuinely happy person.

Jennifer knew she was not a happy person. She had never gotten over her husband's infidelities. It forced her into therapy. It was there that she came to realize how much she hated growing up in a parsonage, how jealous she was of her sister Rachel, how much she disliked her brother Frank, but more than anything, how much she resented her brother Ben.

Growing up, Ben had been the golden child. He could do no wrong and would get away with anything. He was a perfect liar. She knew that for a fact.

She had discovered his homosexuality when Ben was a senior in high school, and she was at the community college. He had everybody fooled, especially their parents.

Jennifer came home unexpectedly one day while her parents were out of town. Frank was off in law school, Rachel in senior college. Jennifer and Ben were supposed to be at school and were staying the night with different friends.

Jennifer unlocked the back door and ran up the stairs to her room to get the notebook she had forgotten that morning. She froze in her tracks. She heard someone in her parents' bedroom. Her heart was pounding. She began breathing hard. She listened.

There was laughter. It was Ben.

She walked down the hall to the door of the master suite. Its door was slightly open. She peeked inside. The laughter was coming from the master bath.

Jennifer silently walked across the floor toward the bathroom door. She stopped. Through the space between the door and the facing she could see the large mirror, and in the mirror, she could see Ben and some boy in the Jacuzzi tub.

Ben was looking at the boy, laughing. Then Ben rose up and leaned over the boy and kissed him on the mouth.

Jennifer caught her breath. Ben looked up. They made eye contact in the mirror through the crack in the door.

Jennifer ran from the room, down the stairs and out to her car. She sped away crying, not knowing what to do. In just minutes she was in the college parking lot.

Her cell phone rang. It was Ben. She rejected the call. It rang again. It was Ben. She rejected the call again, then again, and again.

Suddenly she was startled by a knock on the window. It was her boyfriend.

"Come on, you'll be late for class."

He was with his friends from the soccer team. He didn't even notice that she had been crying. That was not unusual. He often didn't notice her, especially if he was with the guys.

Jennifer buried her feelings, silenced her phone, and wiped the tears from her eyes. She checked her hair and make-up in the mirror, then joined James and his buddies as if nothing had happened. She was good at that.

Later that afternoon she and some of her girlfriends were at the coffee shop across from the college. Ben came in.

He walked across the store like he didn't have a care in the world. Her friends all loved Ben. Everyone loved Ben. He joked around with them a little. Her friend Carissa had a crush on Ben.

If she only knew, Jennifer thought. Then Ben asked Jennifer if he could talk with her for a minute.

She couldn't say no. She walked over to the corner with Ben. He didn't say anything, just looked around the store, smiling and nodding to a few people. Jennifer hugged her books and looked at the floor. She started to walk away, but he stopped her.

Finally, she looked up at him and said, "I didn't see anything."

"You didn't see anything?" he questioned. "Not a thing?"

"Not a thing," she said.

He looked around the room again, smiling at Jennifer's friends. He winked at Carissa. Jennifer looked back at the floor.

"Okay," he said. "I just wanted to make sure."

She looked up at him. He was good-looking and a good four inches taller than her. He looked down at her with his piercing blue eyes. She pushed him out of the way and went back to her friends. Ben left the store.

She never told anyone about that day until after her marriage fell apart and she was in therapy.

It haunted her.

"Jennifer, are you okay?" Lisa asked.

Jennifer looked up. "Yes, I'm sorry, I was lost in thought. Please sit down."

Lisa sat at the table with her.

"You really are a remarkable person, Lisa," Jennifer said.

"No, I'm not, but thank you," Lisa responded.

"But you are, otherwise Daddy wouldn't have hired you," Jennifer said.

"Well, technically he didn't. Bob Burns hired me, but your father worked me over pretty good," Lisa said.

"The one hundred question gauntlet? He's good at that." Jennifer smiled at remembering all the times she had endured questioning. "Mother was even better," she added.

She leaned forward toward Lisa. "Do you really think there was something wrong with what that doctor tried to do with daddy?"

Lisa answered, "I don't know. I felt like it was my responsibility to know what he was trying to give him. Maybe he's just one of those doctors who doesn't like to be questioned. Anyway, I am just the hired help."

"I'm sorry about that from earlier tonight," Jennifer said. "You are way more than just hired help."

Lisa smiled. "I think we can be friends," she said.

"I think we can, too," Jennifer agreed.

Rachel walked up and sat at the table with them. "Daddy is out for the night. Lisa, you were great. Thanks for standing up for our father."

"I just needed to know what was being put in his body," she said. "Thanks for standing with me—you too, Jennifer. Thank you for not leaving me standing there alone."

"The truth is, I was scared to death and could not figure out what the heck was going on. That's typical me," Jennifer said. "I'm not much good in a crisis."

"You're better than you realize," Lisa said. "After all, how else could you have raised two wonderful children?"

"By the grace of God," Jennifer said. She looked at the time on her cell phone. "Oh my goodness, it's almost midnight."

She stood up to leave. "I promised Cheryl that I would help her in the morning with the bridesmaids' brunch. I need to get some sleep."

Rachel stood and gave her a hug. "Sis, it is so good to be with you again. Thank you for all you've done for daddy. I'm so far away I feel like I am of no help."

"It's not me you should thank. It's Lisa. She's the heroine of the night," Jennifer said.

Lisa stood and also hugged Jennifer. "I haven't had much of a family in a long time. I feel like I've become a part of yours."

Jennifer said, "You are a part of ours."

Rachel grabbed both women by the hand. "Yes, you are part of our family, but watch out for Frank!"

They laughed. Jennifer left for the night.

23

THE PATIO

As soon as Jennifer was gone, Rachel looked at Lisa and asked, "What is really going on here?"

Lisa didn't say anything. She didn't know if the condo was bugged, but she wasn't taking any chances. She motioned for Rachel to follow her out the French doors and onto the patio. It was a humid south Florida night. The crickets and frogs made night music on the waters of the golf course. Lisa shut the door.

"We need to be careful where we speak," she said.

"Dad is asleep. You don't need to worry about him hearing us," Rachel said.

"It's not your dad I'm worried about," she said. "He knows exactly what's going on. It's somebody else who might be listening."

Rachel looked at Lisa with piercing eyes, thinking, "What did she mean by someone else listening?"

They sat together on a white wicker couch on the patio. A nearly full moon hung over the lake and golf course. Lisa told Rachel about the drive down in the rental SUV while Mike and Jane were in the minivan. She told about the guy with the wand who confirmed that electronic transmissions were coming from the van.

Rachel's jaw dropped.

Lisa told how Rachel's father had come to trust her. He had told her who owned the house and the townhouse in D.C.: a rich and powerful man named Troxell, and that Bob Burns worked for him.

Rachel's hands went up to her mouth. "Bob Burns!" She shook her head. "I knew Mother never did trust him. I never understood why."

Lisa continued. "Well, I don't trust him at all, and neither does your father. I believe that Dr. Nordia was trying to incapacitate your father tonight, if not outright kill him. By now the good doctor has reported back. Bob will be here tomorrow snooping around. Your father is sure of it. So am I."

"We should call the police," Rachel said.

"With what evidence?" Lisa asked. "Bob hired me, and I'm now certain that one of the reasons he hired me is because I have a record and have been through drug rehab. Who's going to believe me, the former druggy, the 'hired help'?" Lisa said, adding quotation marks around her last words.

Rachel pulled back. "Oh Lisa, I had no idea…"

"Of course not," Lisa said. "Listen, Rachel, your father doesn't want you to know anything about any of this, but I feel like you've got to know. I feel like I am going to need your help."

"Help with what?" Rachel asked.

"Your father has asked me to do something, something challenging and perhaps dangerous," Lisa said.

"I cannot imagine what that could be," Rachel said.

"He wants me to help him clear the name of his late friend, Senator Joe Holloway. He wants me to find a former Senate staff member named Jason Clarke, somewhere out west, maybe in Colorado. He's convinced that this Clarke fellow has information that would clear Joe Holloway's name. He wants me to find this guy and convince him to talk to the press," Lisa said. "And I am committed to doing it," she added.

Rachel stood up and walked across the patio.

As Lisa watched her, she realized that while Rachel looked like her mother, she was a great deal like her father. She had his sharp mind and compassionate spirit. She took her time to carefully analyze something before reacting, just like Pastor John

"You know," she said after a few moments, "This makes sense with something that happened before his stroke."

"What's that?" Lisa asked.

"Before Daddy's stroke, he told me he wanted to come to Africa and spend some time with me. I told him that was wonderful. I would love to have him. I suggested he pick some possible dates so I could coordinate things.

"Then I got a letter from him, a handwritten letter. It was postmarked from San Francisco. He had to have written it and mailed it while visiting with Ben. In it, he said there was something significant he needed to talk to me about when he came. Something he needed my help with. He gave me a couple of possible dates and promised to call soon. The day after I got the letter Frank called with the news about Daddy's stoke."

Rachel turned and looked at Lisa. "Who writes letters anymore? He could have emailed me or texted me; we could have talked on Facetime–who writes letters?"

Lisa answered, "Someone who is afraid they are being listened to."

24

THE CELLPHONES

There was a long pause as they looked at one another with understanding and fear.

"Once we get to the house we have to be careful about where and when we talk. Mike Summers is going to take this guy who is an electronic wizard–the guy with the wand who picked up the signals from the van–Mike is going to take him into the house on Tuesday. He is going to try and find a way to give us a room in the house where we can talk without being listened to. After we get your dad settled in, I'm going to take two weeks off and try to find this Clarke fellow.

"On the drive home, we cannot talk about this. The van is bugged, definitely bugged," Lisa said. "We are also going to need a way to talk without being listened to. Pastor John says I cannot use my cell phone, that I should buy a pre-paid phone for communications, but I cannot call the house. I'm not sure what to do."

"I know exactly what to do," Rachel said. "My African cell phone is too expensive to use here in the states, so every time I come, I buy a pre-paid phone and then throw it away when I return. We can both get phones tomorrow."

"Pastor John also says we cannot use a credit card" Lisa added. "We have to use cash. John thinks Bob Burns can track any credit or debit card usage."

"I don't know that I have enough cash for this," Rachel said. "I use a debit card for everything in the states."

"Don't worry about cash," Lisa added. "Your dad took me to his bank before we left and withdrew ten thousand dollars. He instructed me to give $1,000 to Mike and Jane. I'm holding the rest until he tells me what to do with it. He knows I have to get a phone. He has no idea what one will cost so he won't notice that I get two."

"Okay," Rachel said. "We'll do that tomorrow. I need to get a few personal items anyway."

"And I need to get a few things for the condo and for Pastor John," Lisa said.

"Sounds like a shopping trip tomorrow," Rachel said with a smile.

The next day after the bridesmaids' brunch at the Hilton on Veteran's Boulevard, Jennifer went to the condo to stay with John while Rachel and Lisa went shopping. At a *Walmart*, they attempted to purchase two pre-paid phones. The clerk insisted they had to use a credit or debit card. Rachel asked for the manager. After a short discussion, they purchased for cash two *LG Tracfones* with over 6 and half hours of usage. After 30 days they could throw them away. The total cost was less than $75.

As they walked away from the cell phone desk, Lisa said, "This is fun. I feel like a spy or something."

Rachel said, "Having a cell phone in Sudan can save your life. You're always careful about being in an area with service and about having a charged phone. But some areas have no cell service. For those areas, we always carry a satellite phone."

"I went out one day with a U.N. worker from France. She was new, real talkative, and foolish. We were at a very remote village, outside of cell range. We took a satellite phone, but I said we should still get in and out as fast as we could. She was not at all concerned and wanted to explore the village after we delivered the supplies to the clinic."

Rachel stopped Lisa in the middle of *Walmart.*

"I asked her not to go," Rachel said. "She insisted. One of the workers at the clinic said it would be okay. He would bring her back to our mission later in the day. I took the land rover with the satellite phone and returned. She was never heard from again. That clinic worker didn't return. They believe he sold her to the Sudanese rebels as a sex slave."

Lisa held her hand up to her mouth. "Oh, Rachel. That's awful. You know it's not your fault, Rachel," Lisa said.

"I know," Rachel said. "But I have always thought I could have been, you know, more insistent that she come back with me."

Then Rachel looked Lisa in the eyes. "You be careful, Lisa Smithy. And you use that cell phone to keep in touch with me. America may be more civilized, but even here there are evil people."

"I will Rachel. I will be careful," Lisa responded.

They finished their shopping and headed back to the condo to get ready for the rehearsal dinner that night at the Hilton.

25

THE REHEARSAL DINNER

Once again Lisa and Rachel insisted John use the wheel-chair. He didn't like it, but he didn't protest. Everyone in the family was on edge after the previous night's episode. Lisa worried about seeing Frank again, and about meeting his wife Cheryl for the first time.

She didn't need to. Frank was like a scolded puppy. He immediately came up to John, Rachel, and Lisa, and apologized for his drunken state and his behavior the night before. It seemed genuine.

The *Hilton* Seascape Room was set for over 80 guests at round tables, with a long table at the front for the bride, the groom and their families. Olivia's color choices, yellow and mint green, beautifully decorated the room. Gerbera daisies in crystal vases adorned each table. At the end of the room a dance floor waited before a band stand. The stage was set for a great party.

Cheryl was on her absolute best behavior. A beautiful middle-aged woman, she had worked hard to keep a school-girl figure. Her dress was immaculate, makeup and hair perfect. This was the event she had dreamed about since Olivia was born, and nothing was going to spoil it. Behind the welcoming smile was a fierce determination.

She took Lisa by both hands and said, "I am so glad to finally meet you. From what I hear, you have worked a miracle with John, and you can do pretty much anything."

Lisa didn't know how to respond to all of that. She murmured a thank you and told her how grateful she was to be there.

Cheryl pulled Lisa close as if to kiss her on the cheek but instead whispered in her ear. "Don't worry about Frank this evening. I have him on a very tight leash." She pulled away and smiled at Lisa, then released her hands and moved on to another guest.

Lisa thought, "I'm glad that's over!"

Rachel pulled on her arm. Over at one of the round tables Jennifer was waving. She had their seats. Jennifer, her children Jim and Carol, and Mike and Jane Summers were at the same table. There was room for Lisa, Rachel, and John. No druggy at the table this time, Lisa was relieved to see.

They were all getting settled into their places when there was a commotion at the main entrance to the dining room. Jennifer looked around someone's head and said, "Dear God, I don't believe it."

Everyone turned to look in that direction as Jennifer said, "It's Ben."

At the door with Cheryl, Frank, and Logan's parents, stood Ben and his partner, Robert.

John sat up in his chair. "Ben is here?" he asked.

He looked toward the door and saw Ben. He immediately pushed back, locked down the wheelchair and stood. Rachel tried to stop him, but he was not going to be stopped. John walked briskly across the room without as much as a cane. Rachel was a step behind.

He approached Ben who was by that time talking to Logan's parents. Ben looked over at his father. His blue eyes sparkled, his blond hair was neatly parted and brushed back to one side. On his feet were loafers with no socks, and he wore neatly pressed light khakis and a seersucker sports coat over an open-collared blue shirt.

He was a unique combination of both John and Frankie, but he definitely had Frankie's eyes. For a moment they just looked at one another. Then they embraced.

John wept, but on this night it was for joy.

Robert Schroder, Ben's partner, stood in the background watching as the entire scene unfolded. After a few moments, John looked up at Robert and said, "Thank you."

"Don't thank me, John. This was all Ben's idea. I offered to stay home if it would make it easier for everyone, but he insisted I come," Robert said.

John released Ben and held his hand out to Robert. 'I'm glad you came," John said. They embraced.

Olivia, who was standing by waiting to be introduced said, "I'm so glad Ben insisted you come. I'm Olivia. I'm the one who's getting married."

"Of course you are," Robert chirped as he lightly kissed her cheek. "And tomorrow you will be a beautiful bride. How could you not be?" He was charming.

Soon almost everyone in the room was around Robert and Ben, and introductions were being made. Jennifer stood back a bit. In the past, she and her ex-husband had made it clear that they didn't accept Ben's homosexuality and would not have any association with him.

She saw him at their mother's funeral, but they never spoke. She had not spoken to him in years. Ben saw her and walked toward her. Jennifer could not stop the tears.

"I'm so sorry for the way I have treated you, Ben," she said between sobs.

Ben responded. "I'm sorry for the way I treated you." They embraced.

Ben looked over her head and saw Carol and Jim. "Jim?" he asked. "There's no mistakin' that you're James Pollock's son," he said to the young man he had not seen since he was a small boy. They shook hands.

"I can't deny it," Jim said. "But I hope I never act like him. It's good to finally see you again, Uncle Ben."

"It's good to see you, Jim." Ben looked at Jim's sister. "And this is Carol, little Carol?" he said. He had not seen her since she was a toddler. "You're not so little anymore."

"No, I'm not. I'm in graduate school now, at A&M," Carol said. "I'm glad to meet you, Uncle Ben."

Ben wrapped his arms around both of Jennifer's children. His eyes were glistening. "Jennifer, look at what you have done. Your children are just delightful!" he said with enthusiasm.

Rachel hugged Ben's neck and said to both him and Robert, "We are going to make room for you at our table."

Introductions completed, Ben began walking his father back to his table. Lisa met them with the wheelchair. She locked the chair down. John turned around and sat with a huff. "They make me use this sometimes; something about my getting too tired," he said.

"Exactly," Lisa said. "You've got to pace yourself."

"You must be Lisa," Ben said. "I'm the prodigal son, Ben. I'm sure you have heard about me."

"Only in positive ways," Lisa responded. "I'm Lisa." She held out her hand. "One prodigal to another?"

Ben shook her hand. "You're not… different, are you?"

"No," Lisa answered. "I just wandered far away from home."

Ben nodded his head and started pushing John toward the table as Lisa walked beside. He started to sing.

"Prone to wander, Lord I feel it;"

He looked at Lisa and grinned. He continued to sing. He had a beautiful voice.

"Prone to leave the God I love."

John joined his voice with Ben's.

"Here's my heart Lord, take and seal it;
Seal it for Thy courts above."

Rachel and Jennifer caught up with them and joined in.

"Come thou fount of every blessing,
Tune my heart to sing Thy grace;
Streams of mercy never ceasing,
Calls for songs of loudest praise."

They broke into harmony and began singing at the top of their voices.

"Teach me some melodious sonnet,
Sung by flaming tongues above;
Praise the mount I'm fixed upon it,
Mount of Thy redeeming love."

Everyone in the room stopped visiting and turned toward them. They applauded when the song was over. Lisa said, "That was one of the most beautiful things I've ever heard." John locked the chair down and stood up, and they all held on to one another in a family hug.

Someone was pulling on Rachel's arm. It was Frank.

"Can I be a part of this?" he asked.

"Yes," was the collective answer. They took Frank in.

John whispered to them all, "You can't tell me God doesn't answer prayers."

~~~~~~~

The food was delicious. The conversations were fun. They showed a sweet video of Logan and Olivia as they grew up and came together. Toasts were made, all very appropriate. A few were really funny. Pastor John stood with his sweet tea and finished the toast and blessing he had attempted the night before. It was warmly received.

As the band played and the young people danced, Rachel and Lisa quietly rolled John from the room. They returned to the condo. The evening went by without an incident of any kind. It was perfect.

Bob Burns was waiting for them when they returned.

26

THE VISITOR

Lisa used her keycard to unlock the door of the condo and was startled to find Bob sitting in a recliner in the living area. "Mr. Burns!" She grabbed her chest and caught her breath. "You startled me."

Rachel was rolling John in behind Lisa. "Bob!" John said. "You made it."

"Mr. Burns," Rachel acknowledged.

Bob stood. That all-business demeanor hid a calculating evil.

His great-grandfather had emigrated from Scotland during the early part of the 20th century. He settled on a farm in Pennsylvania and lived to be 91. Hard work was all he ever knew. His nine children were expected to fend for themselves as soon as they were old enough.

Bob's grandfather, the third child, ended up in Pittsburg working in a produce warehouse. During prohibition, he was muscle for the mob. He met an untimely death leaving his wife and three children destitute. Bob's father, the middle child, survived on the streets as a con man and a drunk.

Bob himself was the youngest of three boys spread over 15 years. One brother died in Vietnam. The other brother opened a hardware store in Pittsburg and struggled to stay afloat, but was a decent man. Their mother was a saint who died when Bob was 12.

Bob was like his father in many ways–smart, cunning and ruthless, except he hated alcohol. Getting drunk, or for that matter, getting high meant losing control. Bob Burns never lost control.

He moved to Atlanta when he was only nineteen. He was downtown selling newspapers, peddling fruit, selling beer at the Georgia Dome, pretty much doing everything he could do to earn a buck when he happened to gain the attention of H. J. Troxell, a rising Atlanta businessman who had an eye for hungry young talent. Bob earned his GED at Troxell's insistence and then finished an Associate's Degree at DeKalb College with a concentration in business.

Bob was always good with numbers, loyal to a fault, knew how to keep things private, and would make things happen for his boss, legally or otherwise. He was not an accountant, though he presented himself as one. He claimed to have a small, exclusive list of clients. In truth, he had only one.

Troxell put him to work in his real estate development business. Bob rose quickly, ruthlessly proving himself. He led the way with high tech, high-end developments across three southern states. He developed the planned community and built the demonstration home where Pastor John now lived.

When the boss sent out word that he saw in the appointment of a new Senate Chaplain an "opportunity," Bob didn't need to know the details. He researched and wrote a memo on Dr. John A. Grant, his gay son, and how this situation could be manipulated to create a distraction in the media that they could then use to their advantage. Bob was rewarded with a fat check.

When John and Frankie returned from Washington D.C., John was only supposed to be around for maybe two years. Then his wife came down with pancreatic cancer.

Bob had to wait.

After Frankie's death, John traveled a lot. Finding the moment to poison him took time. When that opportunity came, he was supposed to die, like Senator Joe Holloway did. That would have settled things for good. Only, John didn't die. The high-tech house Bob had built saved John. So Bob had to watch him closely. He did not know what the Vice President told John that night in the townhouse, but he suspected it was too much.

Dr. Nordia was to have completed the job the night before, but Lisa got in the way. Bob's eye for talent turned on him in this caper. The boss was not happy. Bob was not happy.

"I'm so happy to see that you are better, John," Bob said. "Dr. Nordia gave me a report, and Lisa, you should never interfere with a doctor." He pointed his finger at Lisa as he said it.

Lisa started to speak, but Rachel stepped in front of her. "It wasn't her, Mr. Burns. It was me. I didn't like that doctor and was not going to let him give my father that shot," Rachel said.

Bob looked at Rachel, and then at Lisa. He smiled. "Everything turned out okay. No problem," he said.

At that moment Mike and Jane Summers walked through the still open front door of the condo. "Mr. Burns!" Mike said. "I believe you are staying with us. We're in 207, just down the walk here. Have you gotten your things in?"

"It's good to see you, Mike and Jane. Yes, I've gotten my key, and my bags are in the condo. Thank you," he said.

They all stood there in an awkward moment of silence, looking at one another. Many things being thought, many things being left unsaid.

Finally, John said, "Come on, let's get some refreshments and sit down and visit. This is such a beautiful place." He locked down the wheelchair and stood while Lisa got his cane.

Bob said, "No thank you. I've had a long day traveling, I'm tired and want to turn in early. So I'll see all of you in the morning. Tomorrow is the big day! Mike and Jane, don't worry about disturbing me when you come in. I'm a heavy sleeper. Good night."

Bob turned to leave the condo. Then he stopped and said to Mike and Jane, "I hope you enjoyed your stay at the beach." Then he turned to John, "And John, I didn't know you were such a fan of country music." With that, he walked out and shut the door.

Everyone stood in place like they were holding their breath. Lisa looked out the window, and when she saw that Bob had gone on down the sidewalk away from them, she turned around and let out a frustrated sigh.

"Jiminy Cricket, he gives me the creeps," she said.

27

THE NEW SECURITY PLAN

Olivia was a beautiful bride, just as Robert predicted. The wedding, officiated by a judge, a friend of Olivia's, went without a hitch. He did a good job, John had to admit, though he still wished the wedding of his granddaughter had taken place in a church, conducted by an ordained minister.

Mike and Jane Summers hit the road home in the rented SUV early Sunday morning. John, Lisa, Rachel, Jennifer and her two children, went with Frank's son Cole to Westside Church, a contemporary church in Palm Beach, for worship. It wasn't John's taste in church, but he enjoyed the rare opportunity of being with family in worship. Afterward they met Bob Burns and the Streets at Frank and Cheryl's house in Palm Beach for lunch.

Frank was obviously doing quite well. Troxell had indeed set up Frank, John observed. Bob said little and left as soon as the meal was finished. The rest enjoyed their time together.

Soon in the air over Florida, Bob pondered what his next step should be. The upgrades to the house would include video at each entrance so he could not only hear who was there, he could see whoever came and went. He decided to also implement another improvement that had been discussed with Tom, his security chief.

By design, the house could be secured like a bank to prevent unwanted outside entry. Fire code required that each door and most windows open from the inside to allow for emergency exit. The new improvement would be to lock the house down like a prison, where no one could get out.

Bob picked up his cell phone and called his security chief. "Tom, I've decided to implement that other plan we talked about earlier," he said. "Can you get that done on Monday?"

Tom assured him he could completed it all on Monday.

On Tuesday, Mike Summers and his young friend, Will Blakely, the electronics wizard, arrived at the house to do their own security sweep. They didn't know they would be videoed entering the house.

Will identified the bugs in every room. Then he found the control room on the lower level, off the garage. He hacked the computer, then altered the code establishing a backdoor into the system and attached his own wireless gateway. He also made the first of the three downstairs bedrooms secure. When Bob's security guys did a remote system check, it would indicate that the microphone in that room was working, just as it should. It would, however, be a false return. That room was clean. John, Rachel, and Lisa could talk in that room and not be overheard.

Mike spent the time in the study pretending to read papers and taking things from the files. When the young man was finished in about an hour and a half, they left.

In a rare slip, no one was monitoring the new video feed at the entrances of the house, and neither Bob nor his security detail would even look at the video data from that Tuesday for several days. If anyone had seen these two enter the house carrying equipment, they would have been locked in.

PART THREE

The Mission

28

DENVER, COLORADO

Lisa arrived at the Denver International Airport at 2:45 Mountain Time the next Tuesday. She purchased her ticket with cash after driving to Atlanta to visit a cousin. Of course, she had to show a photo ID, but she figured Bob Burns did not have an inside track with TSA. She was right.

She took a cab to the *Westin* Downtown where she had made a reservation. Rachel said, "Don't go cheap. As a woman traveling alone stay somewhere that excels at service. You never know when that will come in handy. Plus, my father has given you plenty of cash."

Indeed he had. Of the ten thousand dollars he had withdrawn from his personal account, she still had over seven thousand. She read the reviews of different hotels. There were three that were outstanding, two downtown. She was torn between the *Westin* and the *Renaissance*. She liked the look of the *Westin*, so she called directly to make a reservation.

Lisa was wary of heights, and the *Westin* had a third-floor room available. It wasn't cheap, but she took it. When they asked for a credit card, she told them she wanted to pay cash. Politely, the reservation clerk said she needed a credit card to make a reservation. Lisa, just as Rachel had schooled her, said she didn't think that was necessary. The clerk said, "Please wait a moment."

A moment later her supervisor was on the call. "Ms. Smithy, it is highly unusual for us to make a reservation with a promise of cash."

"Unusual," Lisa said, "but not impossible."

The man responded, "What if told you I would require a $3,000 cash deposit when you checked in?"

"I would say, no problem." Rachel had schooled her well.

"Wow," Lisa thought to herself after she hung up. "That actually works." When she checked in, they only required an $800 cash deposit.

After getting settled in, Lisa picked up the phone book and began looking for private investigators. There were plenty to choose from in the Denver area. She decided to avoid the big firms and look for a guy in practice for himself.

First, she prayed. "Lord, help me find the right one, one who will help me in this task and not try to take advantage of me. Give me a sign," she asked.

Then she called the first number. No one answered, and there was no voice mail. The second one she called, after hearing his voice, she hung up. It just wasn't right. The third one she called sounded nice. She explained that she needed to locate someone who might still be in the Denver area. He said he was booked up for the next two weeks and could not help her. That was that, she thought.

Next, she dialed the office of Roman Herod.

Lisa and Rachel had agreed to touch base on their secure cell phones every night at 9:00 Central Time, 8:00 pm Mountain Time. Rachel wanted to know why Lisa chose this particular investigator after only three calls.

"Well," she told Rachel, "I was intrigued by his voice. We agreed to meet at 9 in the morning at the *Starbucks* in the River North Art District, not far from here," she said. "That's when the Lord gave me a sign."

"A sign?" Rachel asked. "What do you mean?"

Lisa said, "Well, Roman asked how he would recognize me. I had not thought about that. So Roman had a suggestion."

"'Listen,' he said, 'get the Gideon Bible out of the bed table in your hotel room and sit there like you are reading it. That's how I will know you.'"

"Do you think that will work?" Lisa asked.

"Believe me, lady, no one else will be in that Starbucks reading a Gideon Bible," he said.

"That was it," Lisa said. "That was the sign."

Rachel was less than enthused about the sign. "You be extra careful, Lisa. Be sure who he is, and be careful what you tell him."

"I will," she promised.

After they hung up, Lisa reached inside the bedside table and took out the reddish Gideon Bible, King James Version. Gideon, she thought. She turned to Judges chapter 6, the beginning of the account of Gideon himself, a judge of ancient Israel. As she read, she was struck by how hesitant Gideon was to do what the Lord asked him to do. Lisa could identify with his fear. Tomorrow, this mission that Pastor John asked of her would become all too real.

The Lord gave Gideon several signs to increase his confidence, she noted. She was convinced; using the Gideon Bible was a sign. Roman suggested it. So, the Gideon Bible it would be.

29

THE PRIVATE INVESTIGATOR

Lisa was up early the next morning. Before eating breakfast in the hotel restaurant, she asked the concierge how long it would take for a taxi to get her to her destination. He was amazingly courteous and helpful. When she came back to the lobby after breakfast, he had a cabby who already had instructions waiting for her.

The concierge noticed she was carrying a Gideon Bible as he held the back door of the cab for her. "You going to church, Ms. Smithy? I see you've got a Gideon there."

"Oh, I'm not stealing it. I'll bring it right back," she said quickly.

Jerome laughed. "It's alright. I think the Gideons are just fine with you taking one of their Bibles, especially if you need it," he said with a sparkle in his eye.

She held the book close to her chest. "Oh, Mr. Battle, I really need it," she said.

"The name is Jerome," he said. He flipped a card from his pocket and handed it to her. "Remember, the Word is a sword," he said. "You take care of yourself, and if you need anything,

anything, just call the number on that card. I'll have someone there in a jiffy."

"Thank you," she said as Jerome shut the cab door. She felt like he meant it.

A few minutes later, Lisa sat down in the *Starbucks* in the River North Arts District. She opened the Gideon Bible to the passage in Judges 6. Then she caught herself twisting her hair between her fingers, a life-long nervous habit.

"Calm down," she told herself.

She continued to twist her hair.

She quoted the Bible in her head. "Trust in the Lord with all thy heart, do not lean on your own understanding. In all your ways acknowledge Him, and He will direct thy path."

She had learned that passage as a child. She said it over and over again.

Still, she twisted her hair.

"Why did I get here so early?" she said to herself. "The wait is killing me." She still twisted her hair.

"Lisa?" a male voice said.

She pulled her fingers through her hair and looked up. It had to be Roman Herod. Who else could it be? He had dark wavy hair, dark eyes with bushy eyebrows, and perfectly straight, shiny white teeth. He was clean-shaven, had a pair of sunglasses in his hand, and wore a leather jacket over a gray t-shirt and tight jeans.

She couldn't say anything. A few awkward moments passed.

He pointed at the book. "Gideon Bible. I'm Roman Herod. You're Lisa, right?" he asked.

"Ye..e..e..s," she stuttered. She started to get up.

"Don't get up," he said firmly, but not as an order, more as a request. "May I sit down?"

"Ye..e..e..s," Lisa stuttered again.

Roman sat down. He again pointed at the Bible. "Judges chapter 6—Gideon—Right?" he said.

"Yes," Lisa said yet again, this time without the stutter.

"Do you say anything besides yes?" Roman asked with a grin.

Lisa blinked, shook her head and said, "Yes, I mean, of course, I can say more than yes." Then she came around to herself. "I can also say no, and mean it."

"I am sure you can, Lisa Smithy," Roman responded. "Would you like to get a cup of coffee? This is a coffee shop. Or do you want to get right down to business?" he asked.

Lisa smiled and looked down. She was so nervous she hadn't even thought about coffee. "Of course, coffee would be great."

She started to get up, but Roman beat her to it. "Stay seated, this is my treat. What do you want?" Again, he spoke firmly, but not like it was an order. It was clearly a request.

Lisa had found some confidence by now. She stood anyway and said, "Since I'm looking to hire you, let me buy the coffee. What's your favorite?"

Roman smiled an approving smile. "That's easy; pumpkin spiced latte, grande."

Lisa had never even heard of such a drink.

"And what's yours?" he followed up.

"Just coffee, black," Lisa answered. She was always so plain, uninteresting. She turned, hesitated, and then moved away from the table to go place the order.

A few minutes later she was back with their drinks.

"Mr. Herod," Lisa began.

He interrupted. "Roman. Mr. Herod is my stepfather. I'm Roman."

"Okay," she continued, "Roman, I need to try and find a man who may be in the Denver area. I don't know for sure, but my source tells me he would have moved here less than ten years ago."

"That's pretty simple," Roman said. "What's his name?"

Lisa paused for a moment. "Before I give you any more information, I need to know a few things about you. As a matter of fact, can I see some form of identification? Can you show me a license or something that confirms you are an official private eye?" Lisa asked.

Roman laughed to himself. No one uses the term private eye anymore. He pulled out his wallet and produced a Colorado driver's license and a state of Colorado DORA license as a private investigator. He also gave her a business card.

"The business card has all my contact information and my DORA license number, along with the website for Colorado Department of Regulatory Agencies," he said. "You can check me out there if you want."

Lisa looked over the documents and said, "I will."

"I don't doubt it," Roman answered. "Can't be too careful."

"No, you can't," Lisa said as she handed back his two licenses. Her hand was shaking. "Especially with what I am dealing with. If the fact that I am looking for this individual got to the wrong people..." she left the consequences hanging.

She wanted to look tough and confident. She wasn't sure it was working.

"She is scared to death," Roman thought. "Genuinely scared." She was also attractive. This Lisa Smithy piqued his curiosity.

He decided to play with her a bit. "Speaking of being careful, I would like to see some identification from you. You called me cold yesterday afternoon. Now you are buying me coffee. What is this all about? Who are you?"

Lisa wasn't expecting this. She hesitated a moment, then went to her purse and produced her driver's license.

Roman looked it over. "Hum, Portland, Oregon," he said. He slid the license back across the table to Lisa. "I'm betting you don't live there anymore."

Lisa's eyes gave her away. "That's really not important, is it?" she said, picking up her license and putting it back in her purse, her hands still shaking.

"I like to know who I am working for," he said. "And, whoever this person is you are looking for, it's not about love or a child or anything like that, is it?" He said that as a statement, not as a question.

He looked her square in the eyes, reading her. "You're genuinely afraid; yet, here you are. That kind of courage, it's not for you, it's for someone else, someone you care for."

He sat back in his chair, continuing to look her in the eyes. "You are on a mission."

Lisa blinked and looked away. She thought, "How in the world did he do that? He just read me like a book. He is really good." Then she prayed, "Lord, is he the right one?"

"I have a question," Lisa said.

"Ask away," Roman answered.

"Why the Bible?" she asked.

Roman smiled. That was a good question. The obvious answer was precisely what he had said on the phone. There would be no other person at this Starbucks with a hotel Gideon Bible. But there was more.

Roman reached across the table and spun the open Bible toward him. He flipped some pages and then turned it back toward Lisa.

"Chapter eight, verse twenty-eight," he said.

She looked down. He had opened the Bible to the book of Romans chapter eight. Verse twenty-eight read: "And we know that all things work together for good to them that love God, to them who are the called according to his purpose."

She looked up at him, straight into his eyes. She saw something there, something she knew.

"You are a believer, aren't you?" she asked.

Roman leaned forward and placed his arms on the table, with a smile.

"I want to help you, Lisa Smithy. You can tell me all you think I need to know about your mission. If this guy is here or has been here in the last decade, I'll find out."

"I need to know not just that he has been here, but where he is now. I have to find him," Lisa added firmly.

"I get it," Roman said. "Here's the deal. I get seventy-five dollars an hour, Six hundred dollars a day, plus expenses. Every expense will be documented, as will be my time. If you want a contract, we will draw up a contract. I will need a thousand dollar deposit. Cash, check or credit card accepted."

"Jiminy cricket," Lisa thought. She had no idea this would be that expensive. "How long do you think this will take?" she asked.

"Probably less than a day," he answered.

Lisa looked at his dark brown eyes. She reached her hand across the table. Roman shook her hand. "Deal," she said.

"Deal," he added.

Later that afternoon Lisa got off the elevator in the lobby of the *Westin*. She found two seats and a small table near the front entrance and sat down. She glanced up, and Jerome was looking at her through the glass from the front of the hotel.

He spoke to one of the other men at the concierge desk and came to where she was sitting.

"Did the sword of the Lord help you out this morning?" he asked.

"Yes," Lisa said. "As a matter of fact, it did. I returned it to my room, just like I said I would."

Jerome smiled. His face was full of joy and life, which was sort of surprising from such a strong looking African-American man. The screech of a tire and the sound of a horn beckoned. "Excuse me." Jerome turned around, marched out the front door saying to a cabby, "Hey, you're not going to drive that way at my hotel, no sir."

Lisa watched as a man of Indian or Middle Eastern origin got out of his cab with his arms spread. He and Jerome began an animated conversation. Then Jerome placed hands on both shoulders of the man, who nodded in agreement. Jerome hugged him, and the cabby got back in his cab and moved it.

Jerome turned around, saw she was watching, and gave her a "thumbs up" and a big grin. A moment later he was opening a car door for someone. He was amazing. Everyone at this hotel had been fantastic. Rachel was right. For a woman traveling alone, it gave her a sense of security to have such excellent service. She had a feeling that Jerome would not let anything happen to her, not at his hotel.

Then she saw Roman Herod walk past Jerome and into the front entrance. He spotted her and walked over to where she was sitting. Lisa stood to great him. They shook hands and sat down. He had a contract; she had a thousand dollars cash and the details.

She was looking for a Jason Robert Clarke. She knew the dates he had served as a staff member of the Energy Subcommittee of the Senate Energy and Natural Resources Committee. She also knew he was from St. Louis originally, but the word was he had moved to Denver after resigning from the Senate committee. He was probably well paid under the table for some illegal activity, which would have set him up for a while.

Roman added, "By now that money is likely gone." He was probably right. Lisa hadn't thought about that.

They both signed the contract. He put the envelope with the cash in his coat pocket, smiled at Lisa, then he stood up and walked across the room to the front desk and returned with a phone book.

Lisa couldn't believe what he was doing.

Roman flipped through a few pages. He ran his finger down a column.

"Here it is," he said, looking up. "J. Robert Clarke." Roman pulled out his cell phone and entered the number.

Lisa felt really dumb. Just look in the phone book. She was paying him $75 an hour to look in the phone book. She had not even thought about it.

After a moment the phone was answered. "Hello, I'm looking for a Jason Robert Clarke," Roman said distinctly. "Oh, okay. Well, I'm sorry to have disturbed you. Good afternoon." And he hung up.

"That was Jacob Robert Clark." He shrugged his shoulders. "It was worth a try."

Lisa actually breathed a sigh of relief. She hated looking dumb.

Roman stood, thanked her for her confidence in him, and promised to report back to her tomorrow about noon. As he walked toward the front desk to return the phone book, Lisa found herself praying for him. Suddenly a cold chill ran down her spine. She looked around the crowded room. She felt very alone.

30

TWO HOTELS

Lisa took dinner in her room. At nine central time, she called Rachel and updated her on the day's events. Then she went to bed, exhausted.

The next morning she again relied on room service. Soon, though, she was stir crazy and went downstairs to the lobby. She saw Jerome at the concierge desk and went out the front door to speak to him.

"Ms. Smithy," he said. "I hope the morning is suiting you. It's a beautiful day in the Mile High City."

"I was wondering Jerome, could you make some suggestions for me, things I could see or do?" she asked.

Jerome reached behind the desk and pulled a tourist brochure with a map of downtown Denver. "You look over this," he said, "I'll be right back."

He quickly walked over to a cab that had just pulled in and opened the door. A tall, athletic man got out, followed by a beautiful red headed woman. He apparently knew them, and they knew Jerome. Jerome called one of his assistants over, a guy named Jerry, to get their luggage. Lisa watched as the man handed Jerome a tip. Jerome would not take it. Instead, he stood on his tiptoes and spoke softly into the man's ear. The man nodded. A moment later Lisa saw the man give a tip to Jerry.

Jerome came back over to the desk. "See anything interesting?" he asked, referring to the brochure.

"Yes, I did," Lisa responded. "You refused a tip from that man and instead got him to give it to Jerry."

Jerome looked around his domain and then turned back to Lisa. "Ms. Smithy, I meant in the brochure."

"It's Lisa."

He smiled. "Okay Miss Lisa, do you know who that man was?"

"No," she said while shaking her head.

"That was a former quarterback of the Denver Broncos. He lives in Dallas now, but he and his wife come here several times a year. They always stay with us. As to the tip, he was probably giving me fifty dollars. I told him about Jerry. You see Jerry has a little boy who is really sick. He needs money. I let him work as much as I can, and I direct as many tips to him as I can. That man probably gave Jerry two hundred dollars," Jerome explained.

Lisa was amazed. "Jerome, that is so kind."

"Thank you. I wasn't always kind," he responded.

"What changed you? Lisa asked.

"Do you really have time for this, Miss Lisa?"

She put the brochure on the concierge desk and said, "I've got nothing else to do."

He picked the brochure up and pointed toward it. "You could visit the renowned Denver Art Museum. Just the building itself is worth going to see, designed by some world-renowned architect. Or you could go to the 16th Street Mall and do a little shopping. I can get you tickets to a Colorado Rockies game tonight at Coors Field..."

"Jerome," Lisa pushed the brochure away. "I'm more interested in hearing about what changed you."

Jerome looked down, then looked up and smiled. "Okay. I was a Marine," he said, pointing to a pin he wore on his lapel. "I was born here in Denver, but I thought the Marine Corps would be my ticket out of here, to something better."

"After training, my unit was sent to Iraq. The first tour was really not eventful. On my second tour, things happened. A rocket-propelled grenade hit our Humvee. In the subsequent firefight, my best friend was killed, right before my eyes."

"Oh, Jerome. I'm so sorry," Lisa said.

"Thank you, Miss Lisa. Up till that point I was real cocky. I was the best of the best, and everyone who served with me knew it. Suddenly I wasn't so sure about anything anymore."

Jerome jumped across the entrance waving his hands at a cab driver. "No you don't," he said. "Not at my hotel you don't." He directed that cabby to park in line with the other cabs, waiting their turn for a rider.

He came back to where Lisa was. "There's not going to be any jumping the line, not at my hotel," he said.

"So, what happened?" she asked.

"Well, I went to see my unit chaplain. I had never once attended one of his services. I don't think I had ever said a word to him before, though he went out on patrols, not like some other chaplains who would stay behind the wall and preach from the safety of a secured area.

"He listened to me. I have the gift of gab if you haven't noticed," he added.

Lisa smiled. "I've noticed."

"Anyway, I found the Lord because of that chaplain. It changed my life.

"I came back to the states after that second tour and felt the Lord had something else for me to do. I always wanted to visit New York City, so I went. I answered an ad in the employment section of the Times for a job at the *Ritz Carlton.*

"You know about the *Ritz Carlton*, don't you Miss Lisa?" he asked.

"I've never been there," Lisa said.

"Finest hotel in the world—absolutely world-class service. They have this mission statement. It is just seven little words. Everyone who goes to work for the Ritz has to go through this orientation class. Everyone. They don't have a separate one for management. Maids, garbage men, bell boys, and managers took this class together, and they taught these seven words and what they mean."

"You want to know what those seven words are?" he asked her.

Suddenly Jerome spun across the sidewalk and helped a lady with many packages and bags. She had obviously been shopping. He whistled for Jerry, who came over with a cart to help her get her stuff to her room. Once again Lisa witnessed the same routine as before. She tried to tip Jerome. He whispered in her ear.

Jerome came back to the desk. "You watching that?" he asked.

"Yes," Lisa answered.

"That is Ruth Fowler, a rich lady with a heart as big as the Rockies. When they get to her room, she'll ask Jerry about his little boy. I bet she will give Jerry as much as five hundred dollars," he said.

"Jiminy Cricket," Lisa said. "I'm in the wrong line of work."

"You take care of business here, and business will take care of you," he said.

"Now, about the Ritz. Those seven words are, 'ladies and gentlemen serving ladies and gentlemen.' Now you think about those seven words. It doesn't matter what you're doing —checking customers in at the main desk, cleaning a room, doing maintenance on a toilet, or picking up the garbage, we are all the same."

"I want to tell you, Miss Lisa, those words inspired me. I may have been picking up garbage, but I was a gentleman. And these rich people who stayed in the hotel, though they sometimes didn't act like it, we always treated them as ladies and gentlemen. We were not their servants. We were like them, ladies and gentlemen, only our job was to serve. And we did it, world-class service at the Ritz," he said.

"Jerome, I've had world-class service here at the *Westin*," Lisa said.

"Miss Lisa, those are about the nicest words anybody has ever said to me. Thank you"

"You're welcome," Lisa said. "But I want to know, how did you end up back here in Denver?"

"My momma got sick. My sister was also sick and needed help. I came."

Lisa looked Jerome directly in the eyes. "I'm so sorry to hear that. Are they both better?"

"They are. They are both in heaven." Jerome smiled.

Lisa smiled. "Jerome, you could run this place. Why aren't you in management?"

"That's a good question, Miss Lisa. I started out here doing garbage, just like at the Ritz, but they quickly moved me to the concierge desk. I was good at it. And I began teaching everyone here what I had learned at the Ritz. We added a couple of words to that mission statement. Here at the Denver *Westin*, we say, we are mile high ladies and gentlemen, serving ladies and gentlemen a mile high. Pretty good, isn't it!

"After a while the GM—that's the General Manager— he asked me to do an orientation for new employees. Then they offered to train me for a manager's position, but I turned them down. This is my domain, right here at the front door."

"So you've been here all these years?" Lisa asked.

"Not entirely. They hired a new assistant GM a few years ago, and he didn't like me, so he found some lame excuse to fire me. I had a job the next day at the *Renaissance*. They were glad to hire me.

"Then I had a phone call. Mr. Donnie M. Cravens, the man who owns this property and a dozen others like it across the country. He wanted to take me to dinner. We met at this costly place. He was a former Marine, too. He asked me if I liked working at the *Renaissance*. I told him it was okay. It's a Troxell property. I told him it was not as well run as one of his hotels, but just give me time. Then he asked if I would come back to the *Westin*, as head concierge. Well, the rest is history.

"Miss Lisa, what's wrong?"

Lisa's whole demeanor had changed. She was backing away from the desk toward the door into the hotel.

"Did you say Troxell property, like H. J. Troxell of Atlanta?"

Jerome said, "Yes, I think so. What's wrong?" He asked.

She closed her arms around her chest and suddenly looked afraid. "Where is it? Where is the *Renaissance*?" she asked.

Jerome pointed across the street. "It's right there, right across the street. Only this is the side. The entrance is around the corner."

She suddenly felt like she was being spied on, like someone was listening to her every word. Panic rose from her toes to the top of her head. She thought she might faint.

Quickly, Jerome rolled a chair around from behind the desk for her to sit on.

"Miss Lisa, are you okay?" he asked. At the same time, he snapped his fingers, and one of his assistants got a small bottle of water for her.

Lisa took a swallow. After a moment she felt better.

"Miss Lisa, does this have anything to do with that Roman Herod fellow you met in the lobby yesterday? I know who he is. If you need me to, I can keep the likes of him from coming back around here," he said.

"Yes," she said. Then "No." Then she said, "I don't... Roman Herod is okay. I'm sorry Jerome, I can't tell you what this is about."

Jerome looked at her intensely. "You listen to me, Miss Lisa. Ain't nothing or nobody going to bother you, not while you are in my hotel."

She took another sip of water. She believed him.

31

THE DOSSIER

Lisa returned to her room. She stood back from her third-floor window, staring across the street at the Renaissance. She was sure someone from over there was watching her.

"Lisa, that's crazy," she told herself. But she couldn't help it. That was the way she felt.

Her cell phone rang. She looked at the time. It was just a few minutes until noon. "Hello, Roman," she said, trying to sound cheery.

"I'm reporting in as promised."

"Have you found him?" she asked immediately, hoping there was an end in sight.

"Well, yes and no," he said. "Yes, I have found where he lived, where he hung out and where he spent all his money while he was here. But no, I have not found him yet, though I do have a good lead. That is what I want to talk to you about. I'm preparing a dossier on Mr. Clarke for you, and I thought we might get together for dinner so I can go over it with you."

Lisa did not respond. "He is hitting on me," she thought to herself.

"I'm not hitting on you, Lisa, if that is what you're thinking. I just figure you're probably tired of eating alone in your room. We can eat in the hotel restaurant if you like. Or, I can take you to a place nearby that will give you a taste of Denver. It's called *Steuben's*. I'm going to bill it to you as an expense, so you'll be paying for it. It's not a date, just a business dinner."

Lisa thought about it. He could read her even over the phone. He was intriguing, and she was attracted to him. "I'm here," she thought. "I might as well get out of this place, experience some of Denver and get away from the shadow of that Troxell hotel, at least for the evening."

"Okay," she said. "What time?"

"I'll be in the lobby at 5:30," he said.

Lisa stepped out of the elevator into the lobby at a quarter after five. She sat in the same chair and table where they had met the previous day. After a few moments, Roman came walking in. Jerome was giving him the once over.

She stood to greet him. Roman was in gray dress slacks, with an open-collar light tan oxford cloth shirt. He wore a light linen sports coat.

"Okay, what will it be? Eat here, or go somewhere else?

"I think I want to get out of here for a little while," she answered.

"Great," he said. "*Steuben's* is just four blocks away. We can get a cab—which I will expense to you—or we can walk. Your choice."

"I think we better walk since it will save me money," Lisa said.

"Smart choice," Roman added.

As they walked past the concierge desk, Jerome pulled up close to Lisa. "You still got that card, Miss Lisa? Call that number, and I'll send someone to help you, no matter what. Okay?"

Lisa turned around and waved the card at Jerome. "Thank you," she said.

"I don't think Jerome trusts me," Roman said.

"Nope, not one bit," Lisa answered.

As they walked, Roman pointed out some impressive buildings and one historic spot. Then he told her about the restaurant.

Steuben's Food Service is named for a restaurant that was initially in Boston. During the 1940s *Steuben's* featured some of the best bands of the era in the Vienna Room, the Cave and the Blue room, all part of the *Steuben's* establishment. By the 60s it was a regular stop for the members of the Rat Pack. For over three decades it had been the center of social life in downtown Boston, but it declined.

Some descendants of the founder moved out west and opened a new restaurant under the same name in Denver. There are now several more of these restaurants in the Denver area and elsewhere in Colorado.

It was in an old building that had been upgraded, but it still retained its original character. The menu was pretty diverse: steaks, seafood, different salads, sandwiches and the like, plus a special for each day of the week. It was a little on the expensive side.

Roman was the perfect gentleman, opening the door for her as they entered the building, pulling her chair out and pushing it up to the table as they were seated.

The waiter brought water and a menu for each of them.

As they looked at the menu, he suggested the skirt steak, with *Steuben's* fries and chimichurri butter. "This is a Denver original," he said.

"That looks kind of pricey," Lisa said.

"Hey," Roman said with a wink, "Money's not an issue."

Lisa gave him a twisted smile.

The waiter came over, and Roman ordered the skirt steak for both of them and the house dressing for the salads. "You'll love it," he said.

When asked about drink, Roman looked at Lisa. "I'll just have the water," she said.

"We will both just have the water," he told the waiter.

She was relieved he was not drinking alcohol.

A moment later the waiter delivered two salads to the table with house dressing, and they began to eat. It was delicious.

"Roman is an unusual first name," Lisa said, attempting some kind of conversation.

"Yes, it is," Roman answered.

"Where did it come from?" Lisa asked.

"Rome," Roman answered.

Then he laughed. Lisa did not.

"Okay, my mother was a history major and specialized in Roman history. She taught at the Community College of Denver. She thought the name would help me stand out."

Lisa said, "Well, did it?"

"It got me beat up a few times," he said. Then he put a fork of salad in his mouth.

Lisa took a bite.

"Your last name, Herod, you said is your step-father's name," Lisa observed.

"Well, that's a whole other story," Roman answered.

"I think we have the time," Lisa said.

"You're paying. Remember, I'm on the clock!" Roman said as he took another bite.

"In that case, I want to know the story," Lisa said.

"Okay." Roman put his fork down. "My biological father, John Miller, died before I was born. Before my first birthday, my mother married Rodney Herod, a frustrated science teacher who thought he should be teaching at the big university, not at the small community college. They had two more children, a boy and a girl, and I became the son he didn't want.

"I was about eight or nine when he told me I was not his son. He said he wouldn't have a son like me or something to that effect. My mother told me he was not my biological father, but that I was his son because Rodney had adopted me.

"After I was grown and established in this business I looked into it. He never adopted me. My mother just had my name changed.

"Anyway, growing up was hell. I could not wait to get out. He couldn't wait for me to leave.

"At eighteen he showed me the door. I was cocky and a con man. I started hustling on the streets of Denver. I drifted for several years. Then I got the crap beat out of me one night in a bar fight." He smiled and clicked his perfectly straight, shining white teeth. "These aren't real. Had nearly every tooth in my mouth knocked out. I crossed the wrong people."

"My mother took me in and nursed me back to health. They had divorced by then. She told me I had to find something to do that didn't involve getting beat up. I decided then I wanted to be a cop. It didn't take long for me to realize that I didn't function well under strict supervision. The police academy and I parted company shortly after that."

"Then I met this guy, Joe Arnold, who had a Private Security/Investigation firm. He hired me, mentored me in the work. I was good at it. Joe said I was really good if you don't mind me saying so. After about ten years I went into business for myself. So I've been doing this for over 20 years."

"That's interesting. Are you close to your mother?

"Well, after she divorced dear old not-my-dad, we grew closer. She died about two years ago."

"I'm so sorry, Roman."

"Thank you."

"Have you ever been married?" Lisa asked.

"No," Roman answered.

"Not even close to being married?" Lisa probed.

Roman was quiet for a moment.

"I lived with a woman for four and a half years. She kept bringing up the marriage question, and I kept saying we didn't need a piece of paper to prove our love. I guess she did. She got tired of waiting and left one Saturday morning."

"That had to hurt," Lisa said.

"Truth is, I was more surprised than anything else. I mean, I thought love was all anyone needed, and I truly loved her. I guess some people want more. Anyway, I was footloose and fancy-free at that point."

"At the coffee shop, you directed me to a specific scripture passage, Romans 8:28. Is there a significance to that passage for you?" Lisa asked.

Roman looked at her intensely and then relaxed. "Yes," he said. "And what I just said wasn't exactly true. I was not footloose and fancy-free. When Ashley—that's the woman I lived with for almost five years—when Ashley left, I was not just surprised; I was devastated. I felt trapped and alone. I practically stalked her for a while."

"Joe Arnold, that man I told you about who mentored me in investigations, I finally went to see him. He was several years older and had a family. He was the closest thing to a father figure I had known. I told him what had happened. I asked him what I should do next."

"His answer blew me away. He told me to go to church. He invited me to his church, Faith Presbyterian. I went. I confessed Christ and was baptized. I got to know the associate pastor. He began discipling me. I was changed. I liked alcohol a bit too much, so I quit, cold turkey. After a while, I went and found Ashley. I wanted her to see that I had changed. I wanted us to be husband and wife, but it was too late. She had already found someone else, and they were married.

"I'm sorry, Roman. I know that was heartbreaking," Lisa said.

"Not that much," Roman answered. "I have been at peace with it. Maybe there is someone else, maybe not. I'm content now with what I do and who I am in Christ. I have even taught a children's Sunday School class," he said with a swagger.

Lisa found herself more and more attracted to him.

"What about you, Lisa Smithy. Is that a married name, or your maiden name?"

Lisa finished chewing her last bite of salad, picked up her napkin and wiped the corner of her mouth. "I suppose you already know the answer to that, Mr. Private Investigator."

Roman smiled and lowered his head. Then he pulled out a document from his jacket. He laid it on the table. It was the dossier he had prepared on Jason Robert Clarke.

"It is not hard to find out information on people, Lisa. And people like you are easy to read," he said.

"Well you have certainly read me like a book," Lisa replied. "Why am I so easy to read?" she asked.

Roman took a deep breath. "Because in you there is no pretense. You've been hurt before, deeply; that much is clear to see. That often causes people to withdraw deep inside and to put forward a false image as a form of protection. It's like, if I am the person I pretend to be, I could not possibly have been hurt the way I was hurt. The real you, that person is too vulnerable."

"But that is not you, Lisa Smithy. You were hurt, but something happened in your life that allows you to both accept the reality of what happened, and yet present a pure and true image of yourself. I look at you and see honesty, and I can't tell you how rare and refreshing that is," Roman said.

Lisa felt herself blushing.

The food arrived at just at the right moment.

As they ate, Lisa told him about her alcoholic father and the death of her mother. She guessed correctly that he already knew about her record and her drug problem. Then she told him that she worked for an older man, a retired pastor who was a real southern gentleman. She was looking for Jason Clarke on his behalf. That was why she was in Denver.

Roman nodded. It was true then, she was on a mission. "Why does he need to know the location of Clarke?" he probed.

Lisa hesitated. "I'm not ready to go into all of that, not yet," she responded cautiously.

"That's okay," he said. "I told you before, you don't have to tell me everything."

Roman finished his meal, wiped his mouth and hands with his napkin, and then said, "Well Lisa, I can help you on your mission."

He slid the dossier across the table. Lisa put her fork down, wiped her hands and opened it, and began to read while Roman described the contents of each page.

The first page told about Clarke's origins. He was born in St. Louis. After getting his BS in chemical engineering from Missouri State—top of his class—he interned with a U.S. Congressman.

The second page of the dossier was about his time in the nation's capital. He did well in Washington, D.C., quickly rising from a basic staffer for a congressman to a staff position with Senator Bill Tate, future President of the United States. Then he was hired by the Senate to work for the Energy and Natural Resources Committee, more specifically the Energy Subcommittee. After about six years he resigned and moved to Denver.

Page three was about Denver. He rented a really expensive condo on the outskirts of the city—ski lodge country. He bought a BMW. He ran around with a wealthy group of people.

He had two tickets for speeding and one pretty serious brush with the law about a girl who was beaten up at his condo. He claimed he didn't do it.

He started to slow down a bit. He got out of the condo lease and moved into a much cheaper east side apartment. He sold the Beemer and got a used Toyota. Then an energy exploration company in Denver called HJT Energy hired him.

Roman noticed a change in her demeanor. "Is something wrong?" he asked.

Lisa tried hard not to show any emotion. "HJT Energy. Does that by any chance stand for H.J. Troxell?"

Roman noticed her struggling with her feelings. "Yes. Troxell's corporation has many investments in Colorado, and I would guess, across the entire country."

"So, you've heard of H. J. Troxell," she said.

Roman laughed. "Of course I've heard of Troxell. He's one of the richest men in the world."

Lisa looked down at the paper. How was it that she was so unaware of things?

She looked up and said, "Can we go?"

Roman pulled his napkin from his lap and placed it on the table. "Of course, if you are ready, but you need to look at the next page."

Lisa stood, "You can tell me about it in the cab as we ride back to the hotel. Please excuse me."

She turned and walked toward the restroom. The closer she got, the faster she walked. She practically ran through the door and into the first stall. Her breathing was heavy, her eyes filled with tears of fear. She was trembling. Everywhere she turned there was Troxell. Once again she felt terribly alone, yet also like someone was watching, listening.

A few minutes later she was back at the table. Roman stood. He had already paid for the meal and ordered a cab. He picked up the dossier and caught her elbow as they walked across the room and out of the front of the building. A moment later the cab pulled up.

Roman opened the door and allowed Lisa to step in. She slid across the seat as he climbed in next to her. Instinctively, she slid her hand inside his arm and held his arm. She fought the instinct to lean her head on his shoulder, with no success. They did not say anything during the short ride back to the *Westin*.

Jerome met the cab as it pulled in and opened the door. Roman stepped out, and Lisa quickly followed. She headed straight into the hotel. Roman paid the cab and then followed her, grabbing her by the arm to slow her down.

Jerome immediately stepped in. "Wait a minute now. You let go of her arm," he said sternly to Roman.

Roman pulled his hand back. Lisa turned around.

"It's okay Jerome. I'm okay," she said.

Jerome looked Roman over and said, "If you say so, Miss Lisa. But this is my hotel, and I take good care of my guests." He said that looking straight at Roman.

Lisa reached out and touched Jerome's shoulder. "Really Jerome, it's okay. But thank you, thank you so much."

Jerome took a few steps back, still looking at Roman. Then he turned to Lisa. "I told you, ain't nothing gonna happen to you at my hotel."

He returned to his desk just outside the glass doors but kept watching Roman.

Lisa looked at Roman, who looked confused. "I need to go to my room, alone," she said, her voice almost breaking.

"That's fine, Lisa." His expression softened as he looked at her. "Take a look at that last page, and then call me and let me know that you are okay and what you want to do."

She looked down, then up at his eyes. "I will," she said.

They made deep eye contact with each other for a moment. Then Roman said, "I think Jerome doesn't like me."

Lisa laughed. "No, I don't think he does."

32

THE FOURTH PAGE

Lisa had just settled into her room when the 8 p.m. phone call came from Rachel. She told Rachel all about the dinner with Roman. Rachel asked, "Lisa, are you falling in love with this guy?"

Lisa said, "I don't know, Rachel. I'm attracted to him. He is incredibly handsome and has acted like a perfect gentleman. Plus, he reads me like a book."

"Lisa, he has had lots of experience reading women like a book. He is a professional investigator. I assure you he knows a whole lot more about you than you know about him," Rachel warned.

"You're probably right. Anyway, he gave me this dossier he prepared on Jason Clarke. Clarke was here, came with lots of money, but had to leave town about two years ago with debt collectors on his tail. Roman has a lead on him in St. Louis. The last page of the dossier is his recommendation."

"Well, what does it say?" Rachel asked.

"I don't know. I haven't read it yet," Lisa responded.

"Why haven't you read it?" Rachel wanted to know. "What's wrong, Lisa?"

Lisa was quiet for a moment.

"It's been a hard couple of days," she said, her voice cracking.

"Has anyone mistreated you?" Rachel wanted to know.

"Oh no. You were right about spending the extra money to have first class service. I've made friends with the concierge. He is great, along with all the staff here. It's just..."

"Lisa, I'm concerned about you," Rachel said.

"I'll be okay. I'm just way out of my comfort zone. Let me look at this last page and see what Roman is recommending."

Lisa held the cell phone to her face with her shoulder. She picked up a tissue and wiped her eyes; then she flipped open the dossier to the last page.

"Let's see. He was able to get a forwarding address from a guy to whom Clarke owed money. The guy said he would pay Roman to find Clarke for him."

"You have certainly been good for his business," Rachel said.

"He's recommending that I spend the extra funds for him to fly to St. Louis and trace Clarke down. He thinks it will take less than a day."

"How much are we talking about?" Rachel asked.

Well, we owe him $600 for one full day, plus expenses for a meal and a cab ride. The round trip to St. Louis he says would be $400 with a car rental, plus a night or two for a room in a hotel and meals ..."

Rachel was really good with numbers in her head. "That would total out about $2000. You gave him a $1000 deposit so we would owe him around another $1000."

"Something like that," Lisa agreed. Lisa was not good at math in her head. It would have taken her a while with a pad and pencil to come up with that.

"Well, you're the woman on the ground. What's your recommendation?" Rachel asked.

"That's a lot of money," Lisa said.

"This is why dad gave you the money. Do you trust Roman?" Rachel asked.

"Yes, I believe I do," Lisa answered.

"Okay then, you'll just have to call him and tell him to go ahead," Rachel recommended.

Before they hung up, Rachel prayed for Lisa, that she would be safe, that she would feel God's protective arms around her, and that God would direct her path.

Lisa pulled out Roman's card and dialed his cell phone.

"Hello Lisa," he answered. "Are you better now?"

"Yes, I'm better. I've talked with my people, and we want you to go ahead as you outlined on the last page of the dossier," she said.

"Well, I'm certainly relieved to hear that. I've already bought my ticket."

Lisa was stunned. He could read her mind.

33

THE SECURITY LAPSE

If things had worked as they were supposed to, the human resources Vice President at HJT Energy in Denver would have contacted Bob Burns the day he had an inquiry about Jason Clark.

A few years earlier HJT Energy had hired Clarke on instructions from Troxell headquarters. They were to keep a watch on him. When Clarke suddenly left town, the instructions were to report any contact from him and any inquiries about him.

This little fact had been forgotten. It would be the next day before the VP would realize the mistake and instruct a secretary to make a call to Mr. Bob Burns.

When Bob got the call, he was at lunch with potential clients in a new venture he was exploring. Bob immediately jumped up from his chair. He told his guests something urgent had just come up. They would have to excuse him. He told the maître d' to give his guests whatever they wanted and put it on his bill. On his way to the office, he called his security chief.

"Tom, someone is in Denver making inquiries about Clarke at Troxell Energy. We need to know who that is, now!

"Yes sir," Tom said. "I'm on it."

Tom called the VP for human resources at the Denver company and asked who it was that made the inquiry. The VP said he couldn't remember his name.

"Did you ask for identification?" He demanded.

"Uh," the VP stammered, "no."

"Did you get a business card from him?"

"Uh, no. I just didn't think about it."

"And why the hell didn't you!" Tom yelled into the phone.

"Uh...I..." the VP was really stammering now.

"Do you have any security video of the guy?" Tom asked.

"Sort of."

"What do you mean sort of," Tom demanded

"Well, it isn't very clear."

"What do you mean it isn't very clear? You've got the best equipment in the industry."

"It was like this guy knew where the cameras were. We never got a clear shot of his face," the VP replied nervously.

"What about a license plate? Did they log him in at the gate?"

"He didn't drive a car in the gate."

Tom was furious. "He didn't drive a car, then how the hell did he get in?"

"Uh... we found a hole cut in the fence, out of view of any camera," the VP answered.

"He cased the place. He got in because he cased the place and you're an idiot!" Tom yelled. "When did all this happen?" he demanded.

"Uh, yesterday."

"Why the hell are you 24 hours reporting this?" Tom was livid.

"I don't have any excuses, sir," he said. "I forgot."

"Well, you better hope we forget about you!" Tom yelled and then slammed down the phone.

Bob arrived, and Tom told him the bad news.

Bob was furious. He paced the security suite.

"What about Clarke? We still got eyes on him?" Bob asked.

"Yeah. I checked in with our guys in St. Louis a few minutes ago. Clarke is still at that little house in south St. Louis. It was his grandmother's house."

"Has he had any visitors?" Bob demanded.

"Not that we know of. Our guys are watching him 24/7 now."

"Maybe it's time he went away," Bob said.

"We can make that happen."

"What about at the Grant house? Anything unusual going on there with the reverend?" he asked.

"No," Tom said. "John and his daughter are just going through routine kind of stuff."

"What about the new video at the entrances? Anything unusual there?" Bob asked.

Tom sat down at the computer console and moved the video feed for the house up to the big screen. He ran it back a few days."

"No, nothing." Then he saw it.

"Wait a minute. The day after we installed the video, we've never watched this," he said.

"And why not?" Bob demanded.

"Because you wanted all that done in one day and I had to add an extra monitor and a new video distribution amp to the monitoring system," he yelled at Bob. "It took all day, so we just never looked at it, okay!"

Bob and Tom watched as the video of the day after installation began to run. As expected, Mike Summers walked up to the kitchen door.

There was someone else with Mike, a really young guy, and he had a large case, for tools and equipment.

Bob exploded. "We pay you thousands of dollars to be on top of this place. Why the hell are you so incompetent?"

Tom didn't say anything.

"Get me the audio from inside the house," Bob ordered.

The audio track followed Mike as he used his passkey to enter the house from the kitchen door. Then it tracked someone to the study. It sounded like that person immediately starting shuffling paper and opening the filing cabinet.

"I don't care about that. What else is going on in the house?" Bob ordered.

Tom entered some keystrokes into the computer. The house followed someone else going from room to room, systematically. He started in the master bedroom, through the kitchen, the den, to the study and then to the guest room down the hall.

Next, the person moved to the music room, into the entrance hall, and then down the front staircase to the lower level. They listened as he walked through the downstairs kitchen, the media room, all three bedrooms and baths, and into the garage.

Then he came back into the house, and into the equipment room. There they could hear someone getting out some kind of equipment, and suddenly the recording stopped and then picked back up. But the time stamp indicated a 62-minute gap.

When it started again, they heard the person moving back upstairs. In the study, the other guy joined him, and they exited by the same door they entered, the kitchen door.

The kitchen door video showed Mike and this young kid leaving at the same time. According to the time stamp on the video, they had been in the house one hour and forty-seven minutes.

Bob sat there and fumed. "How is this possible?" he thought to himself. Two security blunders and both around the most significant security risk he knew of to the Troxell empire: Pastor John Grant and Jason Clarke.

"Where is the Smithy woman?" Bob demanded.

"She went to Atlanta to visit a cousin," Tom answered.

"She did, did she? And you know for a fact that she is in Atlanta at this very moment as we speak?"

"Well," Tom cleared his throat. "We think so."

"I want you to listen to me carefully," Bob finally said. "I want eyes on Lisa Smithy in Atlanta, and I want it now! And damn it, I want a full systems check on that house. And as for the Pastor and Jason Clarke, we have messed around with them long enough. Starting with Clarke, I want them both to go away!"

With that, Bob quickly stood and left the room. The chair he had been sitting in slowly turned in a circle.

34

ST. LOUIS

Right at noon Lisa's cell phone rang. "Hello, Roman," she said, "Have you found anything?"

"Yes. I have found one Jason Robert Clarke. He's living in his grandmother's old home on the south side of St. Louis," he reported.

"Have you talked with him?"

"No, you hired me to find him. I've done that. Here's my suggestion. You make your way to St. Louis and have yourself a little conversation with Mr. Clarke," Roman said.

"Will you help me?" Lisa asked.

"In what way?"

"Oh, I don't know," Lisa said frustrated. "I haven't figured out how I was going to do this part."

"Okay," Roman said. "In the morning early, check out of the hotel and take a cab to the airport. Get a one-way ticket on the 8:10 American flight to St. Louis. It is less than $100. I'll meet your flight, and we will go see Mr. Jason Robert Clarke."

"Would you do that for me?" Lisa asked.

"Hey," Roman responded. "I'm working for you, remember?"

"Yes, yes, that's right," Lisa said. "This is business. You are working for me."

"We best keep this on a business level, Lisa. Okay?"

"Okay," she said,

"But yes, I will do this... for you," Roman added, sweetly.

That night during the check-in call with Rachel, Lisa announced that Jason Clarke had been found in St. Louis. She told Rachel she was flying out in the morning and that Roman would go with her to confront him.

"Then I better get to work on the next part," Rachel said.

"And what is that?" Lisa asked.

"Get that reporter from the *Washington Post*, Amber Cole, to meet with Clarke and get the true story on record," Rachel said.

"Oh, Rachel. I am so glad I've got you helping me with this. I can just barely keep up with what I've got to do tomorrow, much less think about what has to come after that. Thank you so much."

"No Lisa, I should be thanking you. My father loves you and trusts you completely. Anyway, I think it's time to tell him what we are doing."

"Why?" Lisa asked.

"Well, he keeps asking if I have heard from you. I have to lie to him, and we know others are listening. I am afraid of something being said that doesn't need to be said in the house. I just feel like it's time to let him know what's going on."

"Okay," Lisa responded. "Whatever you think is best."

"And one other thing," Rachel added. "I also want to call that *Chicago Tribune* columnist, the Spraberry guy. He wrote some pretty ugly things about Dad. I want the chance to set the record straight with him, too."

"That's fine," Lisa added.

"You call me, Lisa Smithy, the moment you finish talking to Jason Clarke. You call me and let me know you are okay!" Rachel added.

"I will," Lisa promised.

~~~~~~

Bob Burns' cell phone rang. It was his security chief.

"Okay, Bob, you are not going to like this. We sent someone to the cousin's house in Atlanta. The Smithy girl's car is there, but she is not. The cousin would only say that she was gone for a few days," Tom reported.

Bob was surprisingly calm. "Well, you can bet she's the one behind the inquiries in Denver. Here's what we do. I want you to get everyone you can in Denver looking for her. And in St. Louis, take Clarke out!"

35

RETIREMENT

Rachel took her father down to the secure room. There she updated John on all that was going on.

"Lisa is in Denver. She hired a private investigator, and he has located Jason Clarke in St. Louis. Lisa is going to fly to St. Louis in the morning and, with the private investigator, try to talk to this Clarke guy."

"Rachel, I never wanted you to have to be part of this," John said.

"It's okay, Dad. Anyway, Lisa needed help. We make a pretty good team," she responded. "Lisa has spent nearly all that money you gave her."

"Does she need more?" John asked.

"Not now. Tomorrow I'm going to call that reporter in Washington, and we'll try and schedule a meeting."

John said, "Let's pray for Lisa." He and Rachel held hands while John pleaded with the Lord to protect Lisa and guide her steps.

There was nothing for Rachel and John to do now but wait. John went into his study. He said he wanted to work on his book. Rachel wandered around the house for a while, continuing to pray for Lisa. Then she had a thought. She called her boss in Colorado Springs.

A little while later Rachel walked into the study. John was asleep in his chair behind the desk.

"Dad," Rachel said as she reached out and took his hand. "Dad. Can we talk?"

John came back to reality. Rachel was staying with him right now. Lisa was out of pocket for the moment, searching for Jason Clarke. He was in the study with papers and file folders scattered around.

At least one day a week he tried to go through just a few of his old sermons, research or correspondence files. It was amazing how much paper he had accumulated in forty years of ministry. Mike Summers often helped him.

He looked down at his lap. The file was dated Apr 23 - WGBK PRESS CONFERENCE, nearly twenty years ago. He had been reading over his notes from his statement that day in response to the Denominational Wars. In the folder was the actual statement, his notes in preparation, and then copies of letters, emails, and clippings from various media outlets in response to the statement.

He looked up at Rachel. It was like looking in Frankie's face so many years ago. He thought, "When I start losing my mind - which could be any day now – I'll probably look at her and call her Frankie."

"Dad," and she smiled at him.

John reached up a hand and gently patted the side of her face.

"I'm so glad you are here," he said.

"That's what we need to talk about," she said. "I've checked in with my office, and they confirmed that I can take early retirement after the first of the year. I think I should. Then I can come here and stay with you."

"You mean come take care of me," John corrected her and cleared his throat. He pulled himself up in the chair.

"At some point, yes. But right now you're doing pretty good. You just need a little help. And a little companionship," she added, with a smile and a turn of her head, just like her mother used to do.

"You could help me with all of this," he said, sweeping his hand across the pile of folders and papers on the desk and the row of file cabinets against the wall.

"I could," Rachel added, picking up the folder that was on his lap. She began flipping through the pages.

"Oh, I remember this. This is that press conference," she said while reading the statement. "You were president of the denomination that year. Daddy, this was one of your finest moments," she added.

John thought to himself; all those years of writing sermons and preaching the Word of God, leading studies and conferences, counseling troubled people, visiting the sick, walking through times of death with so many people—all of that, and his response to a bunch of immature nonsense was his finest moment?

"This is what started all our troubles," he said, pointing at the folder.

"Oh no, Daddy. I was with the Board in Haiti when this happened. I remember reading about it online that night and then watching the video on the station's web page. You were..."

"A reasonable voice crying out in a wilderness of confusion," John said, repeating what had become the response to his statement that day. "Rachel, you cannot imagine what it was like."

Rachel stood up and walked around to the front of the desk with the folder open in her hands. She began to read out loud.

"Thank you for coming today. In all my years as a pastor and as a student of life, I have been amazed at the tremendous diversity that is to be found in everything. The opening pages of the Bible tell of God creating light, vegetation, animal life and human life. And His simple evaluation of all His creative work, three words—it is good.

"What is unsaid but deeply ingrained in the wonder of creation is that it was amazingly diverse. This tells us something important about the creator God. He loves diversity.

"Of course, this great diversity can be and is a source of conflict. Many who hear this statement would not even agree with my opening sentiment that God created it all. And among those who do believe in a creator God, we cannot agree on how He created it all.

"It is easier to accept the diversity that is found in the natural world around us than it is to accept the diversity in opinion—or belief—that is within us. This is an age-old problem. It wasn't just invented a few weeks ago.

"How can people who disagree about fundamental things find ways to live in peace with one another? It is not easy. It has never been easy. Today seems to be a time when such conflicting voices are at a high pitch. Is there any way to find harmony in this?

"I cannot speak for other churches or denominations, and certainly not for other people. I can only give one man's opinion.

"All the sermonizing and prophesying in the world is empty apart from caring for other people. And the real crucible of that love is when it concerns someone with whom you disagree on the fundamental issues of life. In this sense, we have failed. I have failed. My denomination, my church, other denominations and churches—we have all failed.

"When you have a single cause—whatever that cause may be, from being pro-life to being pro-LGBT—and your dedication to that cause results in words and actions of hatred, you have failed.

"I understand that there are issues we passionately disagree on, issues that make getting along difficult, but isn't finding a way to get along the fight that is worth fighting? I long ago got over the need to make others see life as I do. But I do see life a particular way, the way my faith leads me to. I do not apologize for that, but neither will I allow that to cause me to hate another human being. Life is too short, and the planet we share too fragile for us to allow hatred to reign.

"I ask you to join me in THIS fight, not in this nonsense that is floating around today. Every person has to follow the light they are allowed to see. If that light leads you to one church and not another, or even away from church, so be it. If that light calls you to champion one side of an issue and not the other, so be it. I may not see the light as you do, but I can respect you for following the light you have. And all of us would do well to always seek the greater light as it may be found. I pray God will give us that light.

"Thank you."

"Daddy, this was... wonderful. We were all so proud of you," Rachel said.

"Thank you, sweetheart,' he said. "Your mother had as much to do with that statement as I did."

The memory of Frankie Grant hung in the air like an old, sweet fragrance.

"We were partners in everything," John added, his voice cracking.

Rachel came around the desk to embrace her father. For many moments there was nothing to say. Silence said it all.

Finally, John broke the moment. "I don't want you to leave your work, Rachel. I know how important it is to you."

"I'm going to do it, Daddy. I'm going to take the early retirement. I'll be here until Lisa returns, and then I'm going to fly out west and see Ben. Then I'm going to return to Africa. With accumulated sick leave and vacation time, I can come home for good before Christmas."

With that news, John leaned back in his chair and let out a sigh. Rachel was coming home.

Never in Rachel's wildest dreams did she anticipate the shock of the next phone call.

36

JASON CLARKE

The next day Rachel's secure cell phone vibrated. She was in the laundry room swapping out clothes from the washing machine to the dryer. She hurried down the front stairs and into the secure bedroom before she answered.

"Lisa, tell me. How did it go?" she said excitedly into the phone.

Lisa screamed! "He's dead. He's dead. They shot him. Oh God!" Lisa screamed into the phone.

"Lisa... Lisa..." Rachel tried to get her attention. She could hear her sobbing.

"Lisa, can you hear me? Who's dead? Lisa? What has happened?"

Lisa continued to sob. Rachel could tell she was in a car and it sounded like the car was moving fast. A panicked male voice said, "Who are you people? What do you want with me? Why are you here?"

"Lisa! Lisa!" Rachel continued to try and get Lisa to respond.

Finally, Lisa came back on the line. "Rachel, I can't believe it. Oh God, it was horrible."

"Lisa, what has happened, dear? Please tell me. What's going on?"

"They shot him...they shot him. I watched him fall... through the front door. He was yelling at me, he was warning me, to run, to get away, fast," Lisa said between sobs.

"They shot who, Lisa? Who did they shoot? Who was shooting? Tell me," Rachel pleaded.

She sobbed loudly. "He's dead because of me. Oh God, I am so afraid. They killed him, Rachel; they killed him!" Lisa was hysterical again. Then the phone went dead.

~~~~

The morning had started off with no hint of the terror that was to come. Lisa checked out of the *Westin*. Jerome helped her into an early morning cab and wished her well. "Remember," he said. "The Word is your sword." Lisa smiled at him as the cab pulled away.

She had no difficulty getting on the flight, and Roman met her at the baggage carousel. When she saw him, she ran up to him and threw her arms around his neck. For a brief moment, they held each other. It had been a long time since she had been in the arms of a man. They lingered for a few moments before Roman pulled away. "Let's get your bag," he said.

Moments later he put her suitcase in the trunk of a rental car. They drove away from the airport.

"Jason Clarke is living in his grandmother's old house in the Carondelet neighborhood, south of downtown. I've seen him come and go. He is still driving that old Toyota," Roman reported.

As he told her this, he handed her a folder with photos of Clarke leaving the house and getting in his car. Each photo had a date and time stamp on it. Lisa looked them over. "How did you get these?" she asked.

Roman held up his cell phone. "Laptop computer at the hotel. I printed the photos out this morning in the hotel's business center before heading to the airport to meet you. You'll be billed for it," he said with a sly smile.

"Gee, thanks," Lisa said. "Okay, how do we do this?"

"I say we go on out to the house. You stay in the car, and I'll go to the door and tell him someone wants to speak to him," Roman said, in a carefree manner. "When he agrees, I'll wave at you to come in."

"What if he doesn't agree?" Lisa asked.

"I'll make him agree," Roman said.

That sounded okay to Lisa.

A short time later they pulled up in front of a bungalow style house that had to be over 100 years old. Both of the houses on either side of the house where Clarke was, along with several others on the street, were currently under renovation.

The street level was higher than the house, which was on a slope that continued down to the next street. Roman parked on the street with the passenger side toward the house. Lisa had a good view of the entire front. A small driveway sloped down from the street to a one-car garage, which was closed. On the slope was a green late-model Toyota with Colorado tags.

Roman left the car and the air conditioning running. It was humid and hot in St. Louis. "Turn it off, lock it and bring the keys when I call for you to come," he said to her.

"Okay," she said. She watched as Roman walked around the front of the car. He looked at her and smiled, then started down the slope to the front door. He knocked.

The door opened. There was a brief conversation with a man. The man reached out and grabbed Roman by the shirt and pulled him inside the house. Lisa was alarmed. She rolled down her window and heard what sounded like a struggle—like two men fighting, things being broken. Then she heard a gunshot.

Lisa was about to panic. She didn't know what to do. Then, on the far end of the house, a window opened. A man kicked out the screen, climbed out and ran up the hill toward Lisa's running rental car. Just as he got to the car, the front door of the house opened, and Roman came out. He hollered to Lisa. "Run, Lisa! Get away; get away fast!"

Then another gunshot rang out. Roman stopped and grabbed his upper chest. He hollered again, "Run. Get away!" Another shot rang out, and his head jerked to the side. He went down. It all happened so fast Lisa didn't have time to think. Before she knew it, the man who had come out of the window opened the driver's door, jumped in, threw the car into gear, and they sped away.

Lisa pulled out her phone and called Rachel, but all she could do was scream and cry.

After a moment Jason Clarke grabbed the cellphone away from Lisa, hung it up, and threw it in the back seat. "Who are you?" he demanded.

All Lisa could do was cry.

"Listen, lady, I don't know who that guy was back there, but he saved my life. Now, who was he? Who are you?" he demanded.

Lisa stopped crying enough to look up at him. They were speeding through the city streets. She looked back. "Is anybody following us?" she asked.

"I don't think so," he said. "Your friend back there hit one of the guys on the side of his head with a candlestick, and he shot the other one," Clarke said. "You still haven't answered me! WHO ARE YOU?" he yelled.

"I'm Lisa Smithy. The guy was a private investigator, named Roman Herod. I hired him ...Oh God!" she started crying again.

Clarke reached over and jerked her. "Come on, keep it together. Tell me who you are!"

Lisa wiped her nose and eyes. "He was a private investigator I hired to find you," she said.

"Why did you want to find me?" Clarke demanded.

"Because you know the true story about what happened to Senator Joe Holloway. His best friend, Pastor John Grant, wants you to clear Senator's Holloway's name."

"John Grant?" Clarke searched his memory. "The chaplain, the one with the gay son?"

"Yes. I work for Pastor John," Lisa answered. She was more in control of her emotions now. "Those men back there, the ones who shot Roman, they were H J Troxell's men, weren't they?" she asked.

"They didn't exactly say." Clarke swerved around a slow car while still speeding down a St. Louis freeway. "But yes, I am sure they were sent by Mr. Troxell."

"Where are we going?" Lisa asked.

"I don't know," Clarke answered. "Anywhere but here."

"What happened in the house?"

Clarke glanced at her, then got a determined look on his face. He swung down an exit ramp and then into an empty parking lot. He came to an abrupt stop.

"Listen, Lisa, whoever you are. Just get out," he said.

Lisa looked around. She had no idea where she was. "No," she said.

He slammed his hands against the steering wheel. "Listen, lady, I've got to get out of here fast and disappear. Those goons or more will be looking for me. I can't get away with you hanging around my neck. Get out!"

"Where are you going to go?" Lisa asked.

"I don't know," Jason answered.

"They can track you wherever you go. Your only chance is to come clean and tell what really happened," Lisa countered.

"Are you kidding me, lady? That's a sure death warrant," he said.

"You've already got a death warrant out on you, Jason. And it is never going to stop, not until you are dead. Listen, I've got two reporters, one from Chicago and one from Washington D.C. who are just waiting to hear your story. You get the true story out there, and Troxell and his goons go to prison, for a long time," she argued.

"No, no, Clarke said. "I have to run. I have to get out of here."

"And where will you go? Where could you possibly go that would be out of H.J. Troxell's reach? Look, you said my friend saved your life. Well, he was with me to try and get you to get the true story out. You owe him," she said, tears welling up again. "You owe him your life!"

Clarke leaned his head against the steering wheel. "When I came here to my grandmother's house, I thought I had gotten away from them. Then the short one said they had been watching me the whole time I was here, the whole time!" He slammed his hands against the steering wheel again. "They duck-taped me to a kitchen chair and pulled out a syringe and some drug. They were going to inject me with something. The short guy said I wouldn't feel a thing.

"Then your friend knocked on the door. Shorty went over and answered the door. He pulled your guy in, and they started fighting. Your guy grabbed a big brass candlestick off a table—my grandmother loved candles and candlesticks—and bashed the short guy on the side of the face. They both went down to the floor. The big guy who was guarding me pulled out a gun, but before I knew what was happening, your guy came up with a gun and shot the big guy right between the eyes. He went down.

"Your guy ran over to me, pulled the rag out of my mouth, and started cutting away the tape. 'You're Jason Clarke, right?' he asked me. I said, 'Yeah.' I got loose and ran down the hall to find an open window.'

"One of the two goons must have recovered enough to shoot your guy as he warned you to get away. I jumped in the car with you, and here we are," Jason finished.

Jason put his head back down on the steering wheel. "You're right," he said after a moment. "Your friend saved my life."

"Look, Jason," Lisa pleaded. "I found you to get you to tell the truth. It is the only way you possibly stay alive," she said. "It is the only way..." She started crying again. "It's the only way Roman's death has any meaning."

37

LOUISVILLE

About 15 minutes later they were across the Mississippi River on I-64 headed toward Louisville, Kentucky, about a four-hour drive. Lisa called Rachel on the secure phone.

"Lisa, are you okay? What has happened? Where are you?" Rachel flooded her with questions.

Lisa spoke calmly. "Rachel, Roman is dead. Some of Troxell's men killed him. I'm with Jason Clarke, and we are on our way to Louisville, Kentucky."

"I called the St. Louis police after your call this morning. I'm sure they are looking for you now. Do you want me to tell them where you are? Are you safe?" Rachel wanted to know.

"Yes, for now, I'm safe. If the police get me they will take us back to St. Louis. We've got to get to the reporters, first. Do you think we could get one or more of these reporters to meet us in Louisville tomorrow?" Lisa asked. Then she thought, "What day is this anyway?"

"It's Saturday, Lisa. Tomorrow is Sunday. I'll do my best to get one or both of them there. Where are you going to stay?"

"I don't know. We will pick something after we get there," Lisa answered.

"Okay. Call me as soon as you arrive and let me know where you are. Don't use a credit card. Use cash, as before," Rachel reminded her.

It took Rachel about an hour before she got a cell phone number for Amber Cole. At first, Amber thought it was a prank call, but when Rachel put her father on the phone, and he knew details about what had happened, she became really interested.

"I'll catch a flight out for Louisville first thing in the morning. As soon as you know where they'll be, you let me know," Amber said.

"Okay," Rachel said. "And one more thing."

"What's that?" Amber asked.

"Do you know how to get in contact with Jerry Spraberry, that columnist with the *Chicago Tribune*?"

There was silence on the phone. "I prefer for this to be an exclusive," Amber said. "This was originally my story," she added.

"There are many aspects to this story. I want him there, also. I want him to correct some things he wrote about my father," Rachel added.

Amber was silent for a few moments. "I can get his cell number. I'll text it to you in a few minutes," she said.

"Thank you. I'll let you know where they'll be as soon as I know." Rachel hung up.

There was a 9:15 non-stop flight out of Reagan National to Louisville, Kentucky the next morning. Amber Cole booked a seat and rented a car. Then she called someone she knew at the Tribune, got Spraberry's number and texted it to Rachel.

After Rachel convinced Jerry Spraberry that it was worth his time to be in Louisville the next morning, she fell to her knees beside the bed and prayed. She prayed for Lisa's safety and sanity, and she prayed for the friends and family of Roman Herod.

~~~~~~

Bob Burns walked into the security suite to find out the progress on the search for the Smithy woman.

"Tom, tell me you've found her."

"Well, yes and no," Tom answered.

"What do you mean? Is it yes or is it no?" Bob demanded.

"Late this morning she was seen in a car with Jason Clarke, running away from the house in St. Louis," he reported.

"Okay, what else is there?" Bob said.

"Our guys we sent to take care of Clarke, one of them is dead, and the other is pretty banged up. Plus, they shot another guy. He is at the University Medical Center. We don't know who he is, yet. The St. Louis Police are now involved," Tom said.

Bob stood there and tapped his foot.

"So, let me get this straight," Bob said. "The Smithy woman is now with Clarke, and they could be anywhere by now, right?" Bob asked.

"Uh, yes sir," Tom replied.

"And the police are now involved, and they have the corpse of one of our guys."

"That's about the size of it, boss," Tom responded. "But we're monitoring all police traffic, and we've got people out in all different directions looking for them. We believe they are in a silver *Nissan*, probably a rental car from the airport."

Bob paced around the security suite. "This thing better not be slipping through your fingers, Tom. Damn it! You have made one mistake after another. You fix this. You fix this, now!" Bob yelled and stormed out of the suite.

~~~~~~

Lisa and Jason arrived in Jeffersonville, Indiana, across the Ohio River from Louisville, at about 9 p.m. Eastern Time. There was a *Marriot Suites and Inn* in Jeffersonville just off I-64. They pulled in, and Lisa secured a suite with cash. Her suitcase was still in the trunk of the rental car where Roman had placed it when he picked her up at the airport that morning.

Just this morning she was with him—just this morning, she thought.

Lisa was so tired she could hardly see straight.

The suite consisted of a living area with a couch, a bedroom with a king bed, and a bath that opened to both the bedroom and the living area. She told Jason she was taking the bedroom and that she was locking the door. Jason said, "Whatever." She went into the bedroom, shut the door and called Rachel.

"Okay, we are here." She told Rachel where here was. Rachel asked if she felt safe with Jason. Lisa said there was a lock on the door and she was going to use it.

She could finally tell Rachel what all had happened that morning. She cried and talked, then sobbed and talked. Rachel listened patiently. After a while, there was a soft knock on her door. She told Rachel to wait a minute.

Lisa got up and cracked open the door.

"I've got pizza," Jason said. "If you are hungry. I also got a Dr. Pepper, if you want some," he offered.

Lisa thanked him. She had not even thought about eating. She went back to the phone and told Rachel what Jason had offered her.

"Lisa, how did he buy food?" Rachel asked.

Alarm ran through Lisa's body. She ran into the living area.

"Jason, how did you pay for this?" she asked.

"I used my *MasterCard*," he answered.

Lisa looked terrified.

"What's wrong?" Jason asked. Suddenly he realized his mistake. "Oh my God. They know we are here."

Lisa spoke into the cell phone. "I'll call you back. We've got to move." She hung up.

"Get your stuff, Jason; we are getting out of here," she ordered while she threw her stuff back into the suitcase.

"I don't have any stuff," Jason answered. "I left in a hurry."

"Whatever," Lisa said. "Let's go."

They walked out of the room, with Lisa pulling her suitcase and Jason carrying a two-liter bottle of *Dr. Pepper* and a pizza box. In the car, they headed out of the back of the parking lot and then across the river into downtown Louisville.

Jason was driving. Lisa pulled out the card given to her by Jerome Battle at the Denver *Westin*. She dialed the number. Jerome was off duty that night, the concierge desk said. She asked if there was a Cravens' property in Louisville, Kentucky.

Yes. There was the *Brown Hotel* in downtown Louisville. The concierge offered to forward her call to reservations. Lisa said no thank you and asked for the address.

When they pulled up to the front of the hotel, Lisa gave the concierge a large tip and said, "We need your special help."

She asked if he knew Jerome Battle, concierge at the *Westin* in Denver. He did not. She showed him the card Jerome had given her. The concierge smiled and said, "You just tell me what you need, ma'am. This is the *Brown*. It's my hotel. I'll take care of it."

"That's great," Lisa said. "I need this car to be parked somewhere out of sight and hard to find. Can you do that?"

"I can take care of that for you, ma'am," he said with a smile.

About thirty minutes later Lisa and Jason were on the 12th floor, entering the only room available that night–the honeymoon suite.

Jason had seen a *Wal-Mart* over the river back in Jeffersonville and announced he was going to pick up some personal items.

Lisa stopped him. She gave him a wad of cash and warned him. "Don't use a credit card and don't take the car. It's a rental, and they may have a make on it by now. Take a cab. It doesn't matter what it costs. The concierge at the front door will help you."

When he had left, she called Rachel back and gave her the new hotel information. The honeymoon suite was one large room with a sitting area, a raised area where there was a king bed and a large bathroom with a whirlpool tub for two and a shower. Jason would have to take the couch. Champagne was delivered, complimentary. She poured the champagne down the drain. She wasn't going to risk him being drunk.

Jason returned about an hour later. It was nearly midnight. Lisa had gone to bed and seemed asleep. A blanket and a pillow were on the couch. Jason used the bathroom, brushed his teeth with a new toothbrush, and then turned in. Lisa quietly cried as she mourned Roman.

~~~~

Bob Burns' cell phone rang. It was Tom, his security chief.

"We've got a lead on Clarke and the woman, boss," Tom said calmly.

"Where?" Bob asked.

"A little more than an hour ago Clarke used his *MasterCard* to buy pizza and a soda. The pizza place is across the street from a hotel in Jeffersonville, Indiana. My guess is they are holed up in that hotel."

"Well, damn it! Let's not guess. Let's find out," Bob demanded.

"I'm on it. I got a hold of our people in Louisville, and they are sending out two guys who can pass as detectives to find out if they are in that hotel."

"What about the car? Do we know for certain what kind of car they are in?" Bob asked.

"Well, the fellow they shot at the St. Louis house was a PI from Denver. I'm sure he is the guy that inquired about Clarke at HJT Energy in Denver. My guess is he rented a car at the St. Louis airport. We are on it," Tom said.

Bob Burns fumed. "I don't want you on it. I want you on top of it! I want this problem eliminated, tonight!" Bob hung up the phone.

Around 1 a.m. Bob's cell phone rang again. Tom had an update.

"They were in the *Marriot* in Jeffersonville alright, but something spooked them, and they ran. The rental is a silver *Nissan Sentra* with Missouri plates. We've got the tag number, and our people are on the prowl in Louisville hotels looking for that car. It's like looking for a needle in a haystack, though" he said.

"I don't care what it takes. Get out all the men you can. Find that car! Find them!" Bob demanded.

38

THE INTERVIEW

The clock showed 10:25 Sunday morning. Lisa had been up for a quite a while. Jason was still asleep on the couch. She ordered breakfast. Her secure cell phone had died, and she looked all through the room for the charger. She didn't find it. The room phone rang. It was Amber Cole, in the lobby. Lisa invited her to come up. Jason still slept.

A few minutes later there was a soft knock at the door. Lisa looked through the peephole. It was a woman. She opened it a crack. "Amber?" she asked.

"Yes," the woman answered.

"Can I see an ID?"

Amber reached into her handbag and produced a security ID from the *Washington Post* with her picture on it. She handed it through the crack of the door to Lisa. Lisa shut the door. The ID pictured a small framed woman with dark hair and dark, penetrating eyes. The woman outside the door matched the photo. Lisa unhooked the chain and opened it, inviting Amber in. She had on dark pants with a tank top over which she wore a light green oxford cloth type shirt. She carried a large leather bag.

Amber looked around the room. "Jason Clarke?" she motioned to the couch.

"Yes," Lisa said.

"The honeymoon suite?" she questioned.

"It was all they had," Lisa answered.

Lisa shut the door and then walked over to the couch and shook Jason. "Jason, Jason," she called. He stirred. Then he abruptly sat up and looked around the room, rubbing his eyes.

Lisa threw a shirt and some pants to him. "Get up and get dressed. The press is here."

Jason kept the blanket wrapped around him as he made his way to the bathroom. He shut the door.

A moment later he came out with a towel wrapped around his waist. "My things," he said sheepishly as he walked across the room, picked up a couple of *Wal-Mart* bags and returned to the bathroom. The two women could clearly hear him peeing. The shower came on.

Lisa sat and stared. Amber got her pad and a digital recorder out. "You look like you've had a rough time," Amber said.

"They tried to kill Jason in St. Louis. They killed a friend of mine." Lisa was too tired to cry any more.

"I'm sorry," Amber said. "Who did this?"

"H. J. Troxell's men," Lisa answered.

"Wow," Amber said as her mind took off thinking about all that needed to happen. "You guys are hotter than I thought."

"We may be in danger here. I don't know," Lisa said.

There was another knock at the door. Lisa and Amber both jumped.

Lisa said, "It's probably that guy from Chicago." She got up and looked through the peephole. "It's a man," she announced. Amber got up and walked to the door.

"I know Jerry Spraberry," she said. She looked through the peephole. "It's him." Lisa let him in.

"Hi, I'm Jerry," he said with a deep, gravelly voice. "This better be good." Jerry was over six feet tall, probably 220 pounds, with a receding hair line and a five o'clock shadow that looked permanent. He was wearing old jeans with torn-up sneakers and a Chicago Bull's t-shirt. He brought nothing with him, not even a pencil.

"I'm Lisa, and this is...."

"I know. Amber Cole," Jerry said.

Lisa looked at them. "You guys know each other?"

Jerry looked at Lisa, and then at Amber.

Amber spoke up. "We used to be married."

"Oh," Lisa said. She thought to herself, "Jiminy Cricket!"

Amber and Jerry spoke at the same time.

"I took my maiden name back."

"She took her maiden name back."

Amber added. "Some things are best left in the past."

Jerry grunted and started toward the breakfast food on the table. "Bacon's kind of cold," he said after he took a bite.

"You don't have to eat it, "Amber said.

"I can make coffee," Lisa offered.

Jerry and Amber again spoke at the same time.

"That would be great."

"No, thank you."

Lisa stood there for a moment, not sure what to do.

Jerry spoke up. "You can make me some coffee."

Lisa prepared a small pot of coffee. About that time Jason came out of the bathroom wearing the same jeans, a new pullover golf shirt, with no socks or shoes, toweling his head dry. Jason was short and thin with wiry hair that was shaved close on the sides. He had the mannerisms of a dorkish en- gineer. He was probably a big *Star Wars* or *Star Trek* fan. He would make coffee nervous.

"Uh, is that food?" He started toward the food table.

"It's all cold," Jerry said.

"I'm making a pot of coffee," Lisa added.

Jason picked up a hard biscuit and some bacon.

"If you could sit down, Mr. Clarke, we can get this started," Amber said, business-like.

Jason tried to take a bite of the hard biscuit. He looked at it, and then tossed it back to the food table. It landed with a crash. Everyone jumped. He took a bite of the cold bacon. They all looked at him. "What?" He shrugged his shoulders.

Amber turned on the digital recorder. She stated the date, location, time and the name of each person in the room. She asked each one if they consented to be recorded.

Lisa said, "Yes."

Jason said, "If that's what you need to do. Lisa, is there any more *Dr. Pepper*?"

Jerry said, "Can I get a copy of this?"

Amber continued. "Alright, Mr. Clarke, tell us who you are and where you are from."

Jason looked around. Lisa poured him some *Dr. Pepper* and handed him the cup. "This is what we are here for, Jason," she said.

"Okay," he said. "I'm Jason Robert Clarke. I'm originally from St. Louis. I'm kind of homeless now."

"Did you formerly work for the Senate Energy and Natural Resources Committee, particularly the Energy Subcommittee in Washington D.C.?" Amber asked.

"Yes, I did," he answered.

For the next hour and a half, Amber asked questions, and Jason answered them. Lisa was astonished at how informed and how organized Amber was, how utterly detached Jerry Spraberry seemed to be, and how forthcoming Jason was.

Then Amber turned her attention to Lisa. Who was she? What was her involvement in this? Lisa told her about Pastor John and Rachel and the plan they had hatched to clear Joe Holloway's name.

Lisa turned to Jerry. She wasn't even sure he was awake. "Mr. Spraberry," she said.

Jerry opened an eye. "What?" he muttered.

"You wrote some pretty bad things about Pastor John. We want you to set the record straight about his character."

"Yeah," was all Jerry said.

It had been two hours. Amber put her pad down and cut off the digital recorder. She said, "We need to get some food." She asked Jerry to call room service and order something. Jason went back to the bathroom. Amber asked Lisa to step out into the hall with her.

Once in the hall, she said, "Lisa, we need to get the FBI in here."

Lisa's eyebrows went up. "The FBI? Why?" she asked.

"Because these are serious federal crimes here, and you and Jason are going to need protection," she said.

Lisa looked confused. "Protection?" It had not crossed her mind how this would unfold. She just figured once Jason told his story, it would all go away.

"Lisa," Amber said, "people have already tried to kill Jason. And if they know about you, they will be after you. I suspect Dr. Grant and his daughter are also in danger. Jerry and I need time to write our stories, and the FBI needs time to round up all the bad guys. We need to call the FBI, now!"

About that time the elevator bell rang at the end of the hall. Lisa and Amber looked that way and froze. A man in a concierge uniform stepped off. He came walking toward them.

"Ms. Smithy?" he inquired.

"Yes," Lisa answered.

"I'm Robert Hurt. The man at the door last night told me about your special request. I thought you might want to know that just about fifteen minutes ago two men acting like some kind of detectives inquired about a silver Nissan with Missouri tags. I told them to leave. Security then ran them out of the parking garage."

"Did they find the car?" Lisa felt panic in her throat. She felt the hall closing in on her.

"No ma'am, not where we put it. I just thought you would like to know. By the way, I called Jerome. He said to tell you two things. First, the Word is your sword, and second, ain't nothing going to bother you, not at this hotel." Robert smiled.

Lisa relaxed.

"I've asked security to put a man on this floor. He should be here momentarily," Robert added.

Jerry opened the door. "Uh, Lisa, there is someone named Rachel on the room phone asking for you."

"Oh, okay," Lisa said. She turned to Robert and took his hand. "Thank you, thank you so much." Then she turned to Amber, "Go ahead, call the FBI. I need to take this call."

She went in and picked up the phone. Rachel was almost frantic. Lisa told Rachel everything that had happened, that they were calling the FBI and that Troxell's men were looking for Roman's rental car.

"Rachel," she added. "You and Pastor John are in danger. You need to get out of that house."

39

THE HOUSE

Rachel felt better about Lisa after she hung up, but now she worried about herself and her father. Then the house phone rang. Freda's voice said, "There is a phone call from Bob Burns' mobile phone. Would you like to accept it?" John took the call. As Rachel ran up the front steps, she heard Bob's voice: "Something is not right with the systems in the house. I'll be there in just a moment to check on it," he said.

"What do you mean something is not right? Everything seems just fine to me. John said.

"It's nothing to worry about," Bob answered. "Just stay there. I'm going to take care of everything." He hung up.

"Dad," Rachel leaned down and whispered in his ear. "We need to go somewhere."

John sat up in his chair. "What?"

Again, she whispered in his ear. "Dad, they tried to kill Jason Clarke. Lisa is bringing in the FBI. I think Bob Burns is coming over here to finish things," she said. "We need to leave the house, now!" she said.

With that, John stood and grabbed his cane. They took the elevator to the bottom level. Rachel kept wishing he could move faster. They started toward the garage and the minivan, but they heard a car door close in front of the house. Rachel led her father out the back door into the gardens. Opening the back door sounded a chime in the house, but that chime sounded before Bob opened the front door with his override passkey. There was no chime when the front door opened.

Rachel and her father went down a walkway and around to the back of a large live oak tree. John stood leaning on his cane. Rachel called Mike Summers.

"Hello, Mike? We are in the backyard hiding from Bob Burns. He is in the house. We need to execute that plan we talked about," she said. "Now!"

Mike called Will Blakely and told him what to do. Will used his laptop to access the house system's primary code through the wireless gateway he had created. First, he eliminated the file and passkey for Bob Burns. Then he changed the override code.

From the security suite back at Bob's office, Tom saw Pastor John and Rachel exit the house through the back door. Immediately he tried to call Bob, but Bob had left his phone in the car. Tom threw his phone down.

Bob had not come to the house alone. He told the guy with him to walk around the perimeter of the house while he went in.

Bob walked into the den. No one was there. Then he walked into the study, then over to John's bedroom. No one was there, either. He went down the stairs, moving from room to room. No one. He opened the door to the garage. The minivan was sitting there.

Tom listened as Bob walked through the house. Then he noticed something happening on the computer screen. Someone had logged into the system. He tried to stop the hack, but he couldn't. He was now locked out.

Bob's companion moved slowly around the front of the house, and then down the driveway to the back gardens. Rachel saw him coming. She signaled to her dad to keep quiet.

Bob stood in the lower level media room and spoke to the house system. "Computer, identify the last exit from the house."

The computer responded. "I'm sorry, I do not recognize this voice."

Bob was startled. "Bob Burns, 2414," he said.

The computer responded again, "I'm sorry, I do not recognize this voice or passkey."

Now Bob was angry. "77215 Bob Burns, override," he said shouting.

Again, the computer responded, "I'm sorry, I do not recognize this voice or override key."

Bob was furious.

Outside, the second guy worked his way slowly across the front of the garden toward the enormous live oak. Behind the tree stood Rachel and her dad. At her feet, Rachel saw a good-sized limb. She slowly and quietly picked it up.

Will Blakely listened in on Bob's exchange with the house system through his wireless backdoor gateway. He thought it was funny. He smiled and hit the Function 9 key. A menu appeared. He selected, "LOCKDOWN."

The house computer spoke. "The house is in lock-down mode. Security has been called and will arrive shortly. Please do not move." It repeated the announcement.

They heard the same announcement from speakers outside the house. "The house is in lockdown mode. Security has been called and will arrive shortly. Please do not move," it repeated.

Inside, Bob yelled, "No!" He ran to the garage door. It was locked. He ran to the back door; it was locked.

When Bob tried to open the back door, his companion could see him through the window. Distracted, the man started to walk toward the door. Rachel came from behind the tree and struck him on the head with the limb. He folded like a deck of cards.

Tom was still listening but was unable to do anything about what was happening in the house. He thought, "This is not good." He threw his cell phone down and then smashed it with his foot. He grabbed his car keys, went to his car and headed out of town as fast as he could.

Meanwhile, Bob ran up the stairs to the front door. It, too, was locked. Then he picked up a chair in the music room and threw it toward the large window overlooking the circular drive in front of the house.

In building this demonstration house, Bob selected the highest grade of safety glass available at the time. It was bulletproof, shatterproof, and virtually indestructible. It was designed to absorb an impact. The chair hit the window and bounced back into the room, striking Bob on the head, lacerating his scalp and knocking him unconscious.

The security team arrived and met Rachel and John coming up the drive from the back. She told them who was inside and of the thug on the ground in the back. Rachel used her passkey to turn off the lockdown mode and open the kitchen door. Security, followed by the police, rushed in.

They found Bob Burns on the floor in the music room in a small pool of his own blood.

40

THE FBI

Even though it was Sunday, two FBI agents were in the honeymoon suite within the hour after Amber's call. Lisa and Jerry sat on opposite sides of the king bed while Amber and Jason talked to the two agents.

"So you think I was unfair in my evaluation of Dr. Grant," Jerry said.

"Yes, I do," Lisa answered.

"You're going to tell me he is a good, godly man, that he is not homophobic and that he loves everybody, and stuff like that," Jerry said.

"Yes, I will," Lisa answered. "Listen," she turned on the bed to face Jerry. "Pastor John was set up and used by the Troxell guy. You have to realize that. Jason has said so.

"Don't worry," Jerry said, "I think you are right. Dr. Grant was set up and used. I'll do what I can to set the record straight."

"That's all we ask," Lisa said.

After a little while, one of the FBI agents went to the corner of the room and talked on his cell phone. Amber made a call on her cell phone, while the other FBI agent approached Lisa. Jerry got up and walked away.

"Ms. Smithy, I need to ask you a few questions," he said.

"Okay, but first you may need to know that the man who was killed at Jason's grandmother's house in St. Louis was a private investigator I hired to find Jason Clarke. His name was Roman Herod."

"Uh, Ms. Smithy," he looked in his notebook. "There was one body found in that house, and he was a known thug in St. Louis. He was shot by Roman Herod, and Roman Herod is not dead," the agent said.

Lisa's hands flew up to her open mouth. Tears flooded her eyes. "But... but... I saw him get shot!" she said.

The agent scrolled through his electronic pad. "Mr. Herod is in the St. Louis University Medical Center. It's a level one trauma center. He's not dead," he repeated.

Lisa dropped her head down in her hands and rocked back and forth crying tears of relief. After a moment she looked up at the FBI agent. "Can you tell me his condition?" she asked.

He said, "Give me a few minutes. I'll find out for you."

"Thank you, thank you," Lisa said. She grasped her hands together and prayed quietly to herself. "Oh thank you, God, thank you for sparing Roman's life."

She had to call Rachel. She started looking for her secure cell phone. "Oh yeah," she suddenly remembered. The battery is dead. Then she found her purse and pulled out her personal android phone. It was turned off. She started to turn it on when the other FBI agent took it from her.

"I need my phone," she complained. "Give me back my phone," she demanded.

"I'm sorry, Ms. Smithy, for the time being, I cannot allow you to use your cell phone, not until we are in a secure location."

At that moment the second agent, the one she had been talking to, came over.

"Mr. Herod is in the ICU at University Medical Center," he said. "His condition is rated as guarded, but they anticipate he should recover," he added.

Lisa thanked God for that news. For the next half hour she answered questions for the FBI. As they finished, she noticed that even more FBI agents had arrived, along with a man who one of the agents said was a Federal District Attorney. Soon, all the law enforcement people were gathered around the sitting area with Amber Cole, while Lisa, Jason, and Jerry sat on the king-sized honeymoon suite bed.

"I've never been in a honeymoon suite before," Jason said.

"Neither have I," Lisa responded.

"It's not all it's cracked up to be," Jerry added.

41

ICU

By late afternoon they were all ready to leave. Lisa was surprised when she walked out of the honeymoon suite. Uniformed police officers stood at the door and at the elevator. Jason, taken into protective custody, was on his way to Wash- ington, D.C.

An FBI agent drove Lisa back to St. Louis in the rental car. They were followed by a car with two more agents. It was after 10 p.m. when they arrived at the St. Louis University Medical Center. Again, seeing uniformed officers in the ICU at the Medical Center surprised her, but it was a relief. She felt safe. The medical personnel allowed her back to see Roman. He was half sitting up. Thick, heavy bandages covered his left shoulder. A tube protruded from the side of his chest. The left side of his head was also bandaged. He opened his eyes and saw her.

Lisa began crying as she approached the side of the bed. Roman's eyes filled with tears. He raised his hand to her. She took hold of his hand and pressed it against her cheek. He said, "I'm so glad you are okay."

"Roman," she held his hand to her face. A tear ran down her cheek, onto his hand, and dripped on to the sheets.

"I thought you were dead."

"You'll have to speak a little louder, Lisa," Roman said. "The bullet took off my left ear. They say they will have to make me a new one. I didn't like that ear, anyway. It stuck out too far. That's probably why it got shot."

Lisa laughed.

Suddenly Lisa was aware they were not alone. From a chair on the other side of the room came an attractive woman about Lisa's age. She had brown hair and looked a lot like Roman.

"So, you're Lisa," she said.

Roman spoke up. "Lisa, this is my sister; Claudia Herod Carter. Claudia, this is Lisa Smithy."

They shook hands. "I'm glad to meet you," Claudia said. "In all these years of investigative work, Roman never once talked about a client. Today, he won't shut up about you," she said. "You must be pretty special."

"No," Lisa responded. "I'm pretty plain. Roman is the one who is special," she said as she looked at him.

"Well, I'm happy to meet you, Lisa. And I am going to leave you two alone. They allow only one visitor at a time." With that, she turned and left the room.

Lisa looked at Roman with an inquiring look, like tell me about her.

"That's my half-sister. Since our mother died, we have grown much closer. She is a dental hygienist. Her husband is an accountant. They have three wonderful children, my two nieces, and my nephew. I want you to meet them."

"I would love to."

She looked at his bandages and the tube protruding from his chest. "How bad is it? How bad are you hurt?"

"Oh, it's not as bad as it looks," he said. "The first bullet entered my back, missed everything but my lung. It collapsed. By the way, a collapsed lung really hurts."

"The second shot took off my left ear. Blood went everywhere. It bled like crazy," he said.

"It looked like you had been shot in the head," she said.

"I thought I had," he added. "The first guy I fought with, he got the shots off at me. I hit him pretty hard. That's probably why he missed. I took out the other guy. When he saw you and Jason speed away, he headed back into the house. I figure he went out a basement door in the back. They must have parked on the next street down and been in the house waiting for Jason to get back that morning.

"I passed out from the pain and loss of blood. Next thing I knew I was at the Trauma Center and the police were questioning me. I was worried sick about you. I didn't know you were safe until this afternoon when the FBI showed up."

"I just knew you were dead," Lisa said. "I thought I had gotten you killed." She burst into tears, laying her head down on the bed next to his hand.

Roman gently stroked her hair. "It's okay now, Lisa. Everything is okay. God works all things together for good. Don't you believe that?" he asked.

Lisa looked up at him. "Yes, I do," she answered.

"So do I," Roman answered. "It's a good thing that he brought you to me."

42

TOGETHER AGAIN

Two days later, in a private room, Roman's doctors were talking about letting him return to Denver soon. Lisa brought copies of the *Washington Post* with the front-page story by Amber Cole exposing the whole scandal and clearing the late Senator Joe Holloway. She also had a copy of the column by Jerry Spraberry in the *Chicago Tribune* telling how former Senate chaplain Dr. John Grant and his family were victims of a wicked plot. Dr. Grant was not such a narrow-minded, rotten person after all, he wrote. There was even a brief mention of Lisa Smithy, his trusty helper.

The image of Bob Burns with a bandage on his head being escorted into a Federal courthouse showed repeatedly on cable TV, along with images of Troxell Industries offices being raided by the FBI and the SEC, and a half a dozen Troxell people across the nation being arrested. Jason Clarke, given immunity for any wrongdoing, was a hero. As for Troxell himself, he boarded a private jet and left the U.S. just hours before an arrest warrant was served.

Local St. Louis TV news reported about Roman Herod and his heroic action saving Jason Clarke. They interviewed

Lisa outside the hospital at one point. She thought she looked fat on TV. Roman told her she looked just fine. Denver news was also reporting his role in the breaking story.

Lisa said she would stay and help him get home to Denver if he wanted her to.

"Yes," he said. "I want you to stay—I want you to stay for good."

Lisa smiled. Her cell phone rang. It was Rachel.

"Lisa," she said.

Lisa knew immediately something was wrong. "Rachel, what is it?"

"It's Dad. He's taken a turn..." she had to stop talking.

"Rachel, what happened?"

"His heart valve... Lisa, if you want to see him again, you need to come, now," Rachel said.

She told Roman what Rachel had said. Roman told Lisa to go. He held her hand. "But please come back. I love you."

Lisa looked at Roman and felt torn. "I love you, too. I don't want to leave you," she said.

"You have to go," he told her. "We'll have time to figure all of this out later."

"Okay. I will be back, Roman. I promise, I will be back," she said.

Lisa got the earliest flight she could. She had to get her car from her cousin's house in Atlanta and then drive home. When she arrived at the house, cars filled the circular drive.

She entered through the kitchen door. It chimed. Jane Summers, cleaning up the kitchen, saw her and immediately hugged her. She said the family was together in John's bedroom.

Lisa entered the room. The curtains were drawn, and a single lamp provided the only light. Rachel rushed to her, weeping.

Lisa looked around the room. Frank, Jennifer, and Ben were there, along with four grandchildren, Olivia, Jim, Carol, and Cole. Josie was sitting on the edge of the bed.

"He will want to know you're here," Rachel said.

Lisa approached the bed. Josie held a stethoscope, listening to his heart. His skin appeared grayish, his breathing shallow. An oxygen tank stood like a sentry. Lisa took hold of his cold hand.

"Pastor John, it's me. It's Lisa."

He opened his eyes and smiled weakly. He looked so tired. He tried to say something. She could not hear or understand him.

"What did you say, Pastor?" she asked. She put her ear down close to his parched lips.

He said softly, "Thank you. God works all things together for good."

"Yes," she said, through her tears. "He does." She held his hand.

Josie pulled back and looked at John's family around the room. She nodded her head. The end was near. Lisa moved away knowing that his family needed to be close at this moment. They all moved in. Ben grabbed Lisa's hand and said, "You belong here, too."

John closed his eyes. He was surrounded by warmth and love. Suddenly he was aware of someone else holding his hand. He looked, and Frankie smiled at him. They were together again.

The End

Carl White served as a pastor for 36 years. He and his wife Frances, make their home in Meridian, Mississippi. They enjoy visiting with their three grown children and spouses, their five grandchildren, and two grand-puppies. This is his first book. You can visit his blog at...

www.pastorcarlwhite.com

.

www.ingramcontent.com/pod-product-compliance
Lightning Source LLC
Chambersburg PA
CBHW052021020726
47501CB00004B/1169